THE SHERIFF JUST STEPPED OUT. . .

Longarm tried the door.

"It's locked," a voice called from inside. "The sheriff's gone."

"Are you the deputy?" Longarm thought he already knew the answer to that.

"I'm the prisoner."

"What's your name?"

"John H. Handley. What's yours?"

"Custis Long. How are you doing in there?"

"Thirsty. Hungry. Scared. Horny. Apart from that, I'm doing just fine, thank you."

Longarm chucked. John Handley might be a real son of a bitch, but the man had a sense of humor about it all. Longarm liked that.

TABOR EVANS

LONGARM

AND THE
SWEETHEART VENDETTA

JOVE BOOKS, NEW YORK

THE BERKLEY PUBLISHING GROUP
Published by the Penguin Group
Penguin Group (USA) Inc.
375 Hudson Street, New York, New York 10014, USA

Penguin Group (Canada), 90 Eglinton Avenue East, Suite 700, Toronto, Ontario M4P 2Y3, Canada
(a division of Pearson Penguin Canada Inc.)
Penguin Books Ltd., 80 Strand, London WC2R 0RL, England
Penguin Group Ireland, 25 St. Stephen's Green, Dublin 2, Ireland (a division of Penguin Books Ltd.)
Penguin Group (Australia), 250 Camberwell Road, Camberwell, Victoria 3124, Australia
(a division of Pearson Australia Group Pty. Ltd.)
Penguin Books India Pvt. Ltd., 11 Community Centre, Panchsheel Park, New Delhi—110 017, India
Penguin Group (NZ), Cnr. Airborne and Rosedale Roads, Albany, Auckland 1310, New Zealand
(a division of Pearson New Zealand Ltd.)
Penguin Books (South Africa) (Pty.) Ltd., 24 Sturdee Avenue, Rosebank, Johannesburg 2196,
South Africa

Penguin Books Ltd., Registered Offices: 80 Strand, London WC2R 0RL, England

LONGARM AND THE SWEETHEART VENDETTA

A Jove Book / published by arrangement with the author

PRINTING HISTORY
Jove edition / August 2006

Copyright © 2006 by The Berkley Publishing Group.

ISBN: 0-515-14173-9

JOVE®
Jove Books are published by The Berkley Publishing Group,
a division of Penguin Group (USA) Inc.,
375 Hudson Street, New York, New York 10014.
JOVE is a registered trademark of Penguin Group (USA) Inc.
The "J" design is a trademark belonging to Penguin Group (USA) Inc.

PRINTED IN THE UNITED STATES OF AMERICA

10 9 8 7 6 5 4 3 2 1

Chapter 1

Longarm froze in place, afraid to move a muscle, afraid if he did . . .

"Custis? What's wrong, dear?"

He sighed, took a deep breath, forced himself to relax. Only then did he feel confident enough in his control to be able to turn his head and kiss the girl.

"Sorry, sweetheart. I'm . . . or I was . . . right on the edge. Ready to bust. And you ain't made it yet."

"Well, darlin', you just go right on ahead and plunge. Don't be thinking about me. I'm fine." She sighed and nibbled the side of his neck. "We got lots and lots of time, darlin'. We can just keep right at this until I do make it."

"You won't mind?"

"Darlin' Custis, I'm just happy to be here with such a fine an' handsome man loving on me. Don't you know that?"

"You, my dear, are one sweet filly," he told her. He raised up a little to take his weight off her tiny body— Emily was such a little bit of a thing that he constantly worried about that even though she assured him that it was a pleasure for her to feel him on top of her—and stroked her breast and then her side.

Emily Balcolm's skin was pale and soft and utterly flawless. In any spot and from any angle. He knew. He had enjoyed looking at every single part of her and had yet to find anything he could fault her for.

Lordy, but she was a pretty girl. She stood somewhere short of five feet tall and weighed probably seventy or eighty pounds, about half of that being her tits. Emily had abnormally large tits for a girl her size. So big they almost kept her from making a living.

Emily was an actress. A pretty good one actually. She specialized in playing the little sister, and could make herself believable for a part as young as ten or twelve. Of course she had to strap her tits down under her costumes. There was no way she could pass as a child on stage with those magnificent orbs sticking out for the audience to see, but with her binding in place and her hair a cloud of little-girl ringlets, she was a natural ingenue even though she was, to Longarm's certain knowledge, somewhere north of twenty-one.

"Custis."

"Mmm?" He commenced nibbling on her right ear.

"Do it, darlin'. Now, please."

Longarm drew slowly back, then rocked gently forward. He heard Emily catch her breath and her arms closed tighter around him. "Yesss," she hissed.

He felt his shaft sliding deep inside her small body. Her flesh was hot and her pussy tight. Tight as a virgin. But eager. Ready. Delightful.

"Oh, my," he murmured, sliding more quickly in and out.

And then fast. Faster. Driving. Thrusting. Demanding.

Longarm felt the sweet-hot rise of sap within his loins, gathering deep in his balls and flowing outward like an Independence Day rocket to explode wildly in a starburst of sensation.

He drove his hips forward hard, as deep as he could

2

go, and he stiffened as hot jism shot out of his body and into hers. Spasms of pleasure rocked and shook him, flowing in waves that he could feel all the way down to his toes.

Longarm grunted and gasped and tried to force himself even deeper inside Emily. Tried to drive himself completely through her. And for her part, Emily clung to him, pulling him tighter and tighter with her arms and her legs alike.

He felt the muscles in her vagina clench and hold; then she too began to spasm. Her hips bucked and her legs were trembling. "I think . . . I think . . . ohhhhh!"

Longarm smiled. And continued to slowly stroke inside her until Emily stopped him with a kiss and a pinch on one cheek of his butt.

"I didn't expect that," she said.

"Neither did I. Disappointed?"

Emily laughed and gave him a hug. "Now get off me, you big lummox. I want a drink."

"You're too young to drink," he teased.

"I'll give you 'too young,' you big sonuvabitch. Now haul that hose out of me and get off so I can have that drink."

"Huh!" he complained. "You girls are all alike. You have your way with a boy and then just cast him aside."

"Yes, that's true," Emily said with a cheerful grin, her blue eyes sparkling. Then she laughed. And shoved at his chest until Longarm rolled off her body to lie exhausted on the bed in Emily's hotel room.

Both of them sat up, Emily reaching for a bottle of the Madeira that she favored and Longarm for a cheroot and match. He prepared his cigar while Emily poured herself a glass of the wine; then both sat on the edge of the badly rumpled and quite sweaty bed to enjoy their break from a long evening of lovemaking.

After a moment Emily said, "God, you're beautiful."

3

"Women are beautiful. Men are handsome. Or not. But men most definitely are not thought of as being beautiful."

"Says who?" she countered. "To me, darlin', you're beautiful. And I'm allowed to think that if I damn well please."

"Watch your language."

Emily laughed, then swatted him on the upper arm, spilling a little of the Madeira on herself when she did so.

"Give me another minute with this smoke, sweetheart, and I'll lick that off you."

"You aren't serious, are you?"

"Hell, yes," he told her.

The sparkle flared in Emily's eyes again. Then she leaned back a little, tilted the wineglass, and poured a tiny amount into the nest of dark curls at her crotch.

"Prove it," she challenged.

Longarm response was a leering grin . . . and setting his cigar aside.

He grabbed Emily's knees and spread them wide, then dropped down and buried his nose in her muff.

The girl smelled marvelous.

And tasted even better.

"Oh, Custis, can't you stay?"

"You know I can't. I have to change clothes and get to the office. But I'll come back."

"Tonight?"

"If I can," he said.

"Make it tonight then, dear. I won't be here tomorrow."

"You're leaving?"

"Just for a while. The company is dark right now."

Longarm raised an eyebrow.

"That means we aren't performing anywhere at the moment, darlin'. We're between shows, so I have almost two whole weeks off. I've decided to go home an' visit with my folks for a few days."

He nodded and leaned down for his boots, stuck his feet in them, then stood and quickly buttoned his britches before he strapped on the big double-action Colt .44-.40 that he habitually wore in a cross-draw rig.

Deputy United States Marshal Custis Long was a tall man, standing well over six feet in height. He had craggy, weatherworn features, clear brown eyes, and a huge sweep of handlebar mustache. He stamped his feet to settle them into the boots, then buttoned his vest and reached for his flat-crowned brown Stetson.

Emily wrinkled her nose and laughed as she leaned back on the side of the bed and spread her legs wide apart, giving him a look at the wet, pink flesh there.

"You are a cruel woman, ma'am," Longarm drawled.

"Just trying to make sure you'll come back to me, darlin'."

"Never doubt it."

"Promise?"

"Promise."

"Tonight?"

"If I can. And yes, I promise. But mind you, I did say I'll be back tonight *if* I can. That depends on what the marshal has in mind for me t' be doing."

"I can settle for that."

Longarm bent down to give the naked girl a long, passionate kiss. Her breath quickened and when he stood upright again, Emily said, "Keep that up, sir, and I shall not be willing to let you go. I shall lock you away in this room and keep you as my own personal toy and plaything."

"Hmm. That sounds like pretty nice work. What say we discuss that when I get back."

"Tonight," she said, batting her eyes and affecting to

look prim and proper. Which was not an easy feat when she was bare-ass naked and sitting with her legs spread.

"If I can," he repeated. "Now I gotta go. Really." He leaned down and gave her another kiss, a very brief one this time, and strode across the room for the door.

Chapter 2

The Federal Building on Colfax Avenue was only a brisk twenty-minute walk from the Fairleigh Hotel, where Emily's manager always housed the troupe when they were playing in Denver.

Longarm rather liked the Fairleigh. Oh, sure, it was seedy and ugly and cheap. But the desk clerks kept their thoughts to themselves. Longarm doubted an eyebrow would be raised if someone paraded two naked midgets and a donkey into their room. It was that kind of place, bless them. No wonder he liked it so much.

Longarm set off from the hotel in plenty of time to make it to work on the very stroke of what passed for an official starting time. He was even a few minutes early. Or would have been if he hadn't stopped for coffee and sweet rolls. Then to buy some matches. And a newspaper. And to have a friendly word with the cripple who'd lost both legs at Gettysburg and now sold pencils on a street corner to eke out a livelihood.

As a result of his meanderings, he did not quite make it on time. When he did amble into the office a half hour or so late, U.S. Marshal Billy Vail's clerk, Henry, looked up with a sigh and said, "He asked for you, Long. You're late, you know."

"Damn. What'd you tell him?"

"I said you'd gone out to buy a newspaper."

Longarm grinned. "Good thing I've got one then, isn't it."

Henry reached beneath his desk and produced an identical copy of the *Rocky Mountain News* that he showed to Longarm, then shoved out of sight again.

"Thanks, pal."

"Go on in. He's waiting for you."

Longarm left his hat on the rack in the corner, then tapped lightly on the door to the marshal's private office.

"Come."

Longarm strode in as if nothing could possibly be wrong on a morning so pleasant. He found his boss seated behind his huge but always tidy desk. Billy looked like a proper businessman or politician, sitting there wearing coat and tie, freshly shaved and smelling of bay rum. The man had round, cherubic cheeks and a bald dome. He was aging now and gave the impression of being every child's grandfather, always gentle and patient and understanding. Probably did not even know any cuss words. And butter would not melt in his mouth. Yeah, sure.

That was what he looked like now. Longarm happened to know that U.S. Marshal Billy Vail used to be a very rough and effective Texas Ranger. He was no stranger to the smell of gun smoke, and could hold his own with a knife or a tomahawk too, and there were a good many men languishing in this prison or that who'd thought they could take that chubby little fellow with the badge on his chest. They had been wrong then and would still be wrong now.

Billy Vail was tied to his desk most of the time, but he was not above dragging iron and walking into the middle of a gunfight if or when the occasion arose. Longarm liked him. More, Longarm respected the man, and that was an accolade he did not give to just anyone. It had to be earned. Billy Vail had long since earned it.

"Henry said you wanted to see me?"

"I do. I have an assignment for you."

Longarm helped himself to a seat in front of Billy's desk. He was hankering for a cheroot, but the smoke bothered Billy. It could just be that this would not be the best time to light up. Still, he surely did want a smoke. His hand strayed toward the lapel of his coat.

"Leave it," Billy said. "I won't be keeping you in here very long, Deputy. You can wait a few minutes before you start breathing the fumes from some burning piece of rope."

"Billy, now you know—"

"Be quiet, Custis. I know. Your cigars are made from the finest hand-picked tobacco. They are practically national treasures." Billy leaned back in his chair, wisps of white hair around the crown of his balding head catching the light from his office window and giving him a halo. "They still smell like burnt rope. Hemp that has been cured in donkey manure at that."

"Yes, sir." Longarm put his hand down in his lap and toyed with the buckle on his gun belt.

"Thank you. Now as I was about to say, I have an assignment for you."

"Something interesting, Boss?"

"Sorry, no. Nothing exciting. It is prisoner-transport duty."

Longarm made a sour face.

"I know. I didn't like that any better than you do, but someone has to do it." Billy permitted himself a small smile. "As the old saying goes, Custis, better you than me."

"Yes, sir."

"Are you familiar with Jack Handley?"

"The name don't ring no bells."

"Handley was arrested in Dakota Territory on charges of rape and sodomy."

"Sounds like a nice enough fella," Longarm said in a dry tone.

"A prince among men," Billy agreed. "He was tried in a territorial court and sentenced to twenty-five years."

"I'd say the son of a bitch got off easy."

"So far," Billy said, "but he is also wanted for the murder of a postal agent in Manitou. He will be arraigned in state court in Colorado Springs and tried there. If convicted—and there is no lack of witnesses—he will hang on that charge. It is our job—in this case, your job—to transport him from Edwardsville, Dakota Territory, to Colorado Springs."

"Where the hell is Edwardsville?"

"I have no idea. But I have every confidence that a man of your keen intellect will find it."

"In other words, I should maybe look at a map?"

Billy nodded. "Exactly."

"Do I have to take that damned wagon, Boss? You know I hate that thing. Damn things stand out like a big old pus-filled boil on a fancy whore's tit."

"I know, but that is the order that has come down from the attorney general."

"If those boys down in the Indian Nations would quit losing prisoners to drunken relatives, we wouldn't have to put up with this shit. Dammit, Billy, I can transport a prisoner just fine on horseback. I don't need to drag a damn cage along with me."

"I'm sorry, Deputy, but I have no more latitude about this than you do. The policy is that a prison wagon will be used for the transport of potentially dangerous prisoners. No exceptions."

"Hell, Billy, this Handley fella wouldn't be danger-

10

ous. Not t' me, he wouldn't. I'd just make it plain that if he fucks up, I shoot him and carry him the rest o' the way draped over his horse instead of in the saddle. He'd settle down real nice. They always do."

"Sorry, Longarm. No deal. You drive the wagon."

"Shit," Longarm grumbled. His hand slid inside his coat practically without him even noticing. He brought out a cheroot, nipped off the twist with his teeth, and spit the bit of dry tobacco into his hand, then struck a match and lighted the cheroot. Billy did not say a word about the cigar this time.

"Henry has the extradition papers ready for you, Custis, expense vouchers, all the usual items."

"Shit," Longarm repeated.

"Have a nice trip, Deputy."

"When, uh, how soon do I have to be there?" He was thinking about enjoying one more night with Emily before he left.

"There is no huge rush. I understand the state court arraignment will not be scheduled until Handley is in their physical custody."

"All right, thanks."

"What are you planning, Custis? I know you. You're up to something here."

"Nothing, Boss. I'm gonna go get my traveling gear, then sign for that damned prison wagon an' off I'll go."

"I do not believe you, Custis."

Longarm affected a look of wounded innocence. "Boss! C'mon. I'm gonna get that wagon an' leave today. You can check up on me if you like. You'll see." And if his first day of travel with the stinking sonuvabitch prison wagon took him no further than the Fairleigh Hotel, well, there would be no harm done.

"If you say so."

Longarm grinned. "See you when I get back, Billy. But next time find me something interesting t' do, would you?"

11

"Get out of here, Longarm. I have work to do."

Longarm surely did like Billy Vail. He surely did. Why, his mood was practically tip-top when he went out to draw his papers from Henry so he could get on with this deal.

Chapter 3

"Custis, whatever are you doing with that . . . that thing?" Emily was staring at the odd rig Longarm was driving. The prison wagon was an ordinary enough outfit but with one exception.

The wagon bed held a tall cage made of welded steel bars, those bars covering the floor and roof as well as all four sides. There was a door at the back, also fashioned from stout bars, with a huge padlock securing it against tampering.

The key to that lock rested now in Longarm's vest pocket, secured to the same end of his watch chain as the small but lethal derringer he carried there. He damn sure did not want to lose that key; without it . . . he did not know what in hell he would do if he found himself unable to open the cage door. A fellow could always pass food or a cup of water between the bars, but there was no way you could put a pail in there if the prisoner needed to take a crap or puke or something, not without opening the door. Yes, sir, that key was important.

"It's my new transportation," Longarm said. "The fella was selling it cheap, so what could I do, huh?"

Emily gave him a skeptical look. Longarm sat there

on the seat with a perfectly straight face. Then the girl broke into laughter.

"Where can I park this ugly sonuvabitch?" Longarm drawled.

It took Emily a moment to get her composure back. Finally, she managed to quit laughing and straighten up. "You make my sides hurt, I was laughing that hard, damn you."

"Sorry 'bout that."

"You don't sound very sorry."

"That's because I'm not particularly sorry. But at least I am being polite."

"For a change," Emily said. "There is a barn around back that guests can use. I suppose you can park that monstrosity next to it."

"It won't take long for me t' get these horses settled. Soon as I'm done, we can go up an' have us a little afternoon delight, then afterward I'll squire you t' the best eating in Denver."

"Oh, my. Do I need to borrow a fancy gown from the costume trunk?"

"I said the best eating, sweetheart, not the finest dining. The place I have in mind, you could show up wearing burlap an' gum-rubber boots and nobody'd blink an eye. But I promise you, you are gonna like the food there."

"I'll be waiting for you, darlin'." Emily turned and scurried back inside the hotel. Longarm picked up the driving lines and took the prison wagon around to the back of the place where at least it would be out of sight from the street.

"Do you like this?"

"Yes." His answer was as much moan as it was speech. "Yes, dammit, I do."

"And this?"

14

Longarm groaned.

"Or this?"

"Oh, my," he mumbled.

Emily looked up, her lips and chin shiny with spittle. And the head of his cock was gleaming with that same moisture. She grinned and gave him an impish wink.

"You," he said, "are good. Damn good."

"Why, thank you, sir."

"Fine. Now be quiet and, um, go back to what you were doin'."

Emily laughed. And began once again to lick his cock. After only a moment, she stopped and looked up again. "I'm having trouble down here."

"What's the matter?"

"It keeps jumping up and down."

"That," he said, "is your own fault. When your tongue hits that one spot . . . oh, yeah, that one . . . when you hit that spot it just natur'ly wants to bounce."

"It feels good?"

"It feels better'n good."

"Do you want me to do some more?"

"Oh, yeah. Yes, I most surely do."

"Do you want me to drink your juice, darlin'?"

"You've never done that before. Not with me you haven't."

"I want to taste it," Emily said. "I want to feel it squirt into my mouth and run down my throat. And I want to suck every last drop out of you, darlin', and get the flavor of it in my mouth so that all evening long while we are sitting prim and proper in that restaurant you said you will take me to, I want to sit there and smile and when I do, when you look over and see that particular look on my face, I want you to know that I am still tasting your juice in my mouth. I want that, darlin'. I really do."

Longarm did not answer. Not with words. He simply

dropped his head back onto the pillow and gently brushed Emily's little-girl curls while the pretty little in-génue bent her lips to him and took his cock into the warmth of her mouth.

Chapter 4

Emily lay curled up tight against him, as content as a cat on a hearth, gently twirling one finger through the hair on his chest. He glanced down and was pleased to see that she was smiling. She was a helluva girl this one. Cute too. He touched the tip of her nose, then laughed when both of her eyes followed his finger, making her cross-eyed . . . but still just as cute as a button.

Both were utterly sated. They'd made love through the afternoon, eaten hugely, then returned to the Fairleigh and gotten happily naked again. Now the lamp in Emily's room was nearly empty, the flame guttering and softly popping.

He really should blow it out, Longarm thought, to keep it from charring the wick.

But that would mean he would have to actually move, wouldn't it. And he was so very comfortable. He yawned, the shadows on the wall dancing with the uncertainty of the flame. The hell with it. It wasn't his damn wick.

"Are you awake, darlin'?"

"Barely."

"Me too." Emily sighed. "Lucky for me the stage doesn't leave until almost noon."

"Where do your folks live?" He lightly stroked her back and shoulders.

"Dakota Territory."

"What?"

"Oh, don't give me that look. I'm a grown-up girl. In case you hadn't noticed. I can cuss and drink and smoke and everything if I want to."

"Well, I'm glad we cleared that right up."

"Seriously," she said, "my folks' place isn't . . . I'm tempted to say it isn't anywhere. But that couldn't be right 'cause everything has to be someplace. It's just that their place isn't exactly close to anything. The nearest post office is a little country crossroads store called Harper's."

"And that would be where? More or less."

"It's between two little towns you never heard of, neither one of them big enough to get up a poker game if any one person has gone off to shop in the big city. One of them is called Cory. The other is Edwardsville."

"No shit. Edwardsville?"

"I told you you wouldn't ever have heard of it." She pressed her nose into his armpit and sighed again.

"Heard of it? Hellfire, girl, I'm heading up there with that wagon tomorrow. Got t' pick up a prisoner an' drag him back to civilization for trial."

Emily's head popped up. "You're kidding me, right?"

"No, I'm serious. Edwardsville is big enough to have a town constable at the very least an' a jail to lock up his prisoners in. I know that for a fact because that's where I have to go for this fella."

"Goodness. It's a small world, isn't it?"

"Sure is," he agreed.

"Custis, dear, would you do me a big favor?"

"If I can, sweet thing."

"Would you please shut the hell up so I can go to sleep?" She smiled. "You have me purely worn out, darlin', and I want to sleep now if you don't mind."

"Sounds like a pretty fair idea." He bent down to kiss the tip of her nose. "G'night, Em." She did not answer. Her breathing had already slowed and just that quickly she was asleep.

"But I'm telling you, Custis, it makes perfect sense if you will just think about it."

"No, dammit."

"Please, Custis. *Please!*"

"No."

"But darlin', you just don't know how things are there. There is no regular coach service so I have to travel to a stupid little town about forty-some miles from my folks. Then I have to wait around asking for the next freight wagon going in that direction."

"What about the mail coach?" Longarm asked.

Emily snorted and made a face. "That old son of a bitch!" She made her voice into a low growl. "United States govern-damn-ment property, missy. It's ag'in the rules." She snorted again. "The old bastard. I hope his dick rots and falls off."

"You were not pleased with him," Longarm suggested.

"You could say that."

"You know, of course, that the wagon out there is also U.S. government property."

"But you are not an idiot like Mr. Baker is."

"Ah, so you know the gentleman."

"Yes, and he knows me. The shithead."

"Is there something you aren't telling me about this Baker fella?"

"Not really, but there is something I've never told anyone. Not even my mama, and I tell her everything." She giggled. "Well, almost."

"An' what would that be? That you haven't told your mama, that is."

"It is what I had to do to get a ride home that time Mr. Baker wouldn't take me. I rode with a pair of smelly old men on a freight wagon. And I had to pay my way. I expected that. I didn't like it, but I expected it. It is simply what a girl must do sometimes."

"Oh?" Longarm's eyebrows went up, right along with his curiosity.

"I mean, the blow jobs were not any worse than I expected. At least they were willing to wash their things before I did them. But then that wasn't enough and they made me do them again after a few miles but with my pussy, not my mouth. And I caught the crabs, Custis. It was awful.

"When I got home, I had to mix up some turpentine and naphtha and cut all my pretty hair and paint that goo all over. It killed the nits, but I like to scratched myself to death until it did."

"Doctors have pastes for that sort of thing, you know."

"Yes, I do know, but then my folks would have known too, and it was not information that I particularly wanted to share with them."

"Emily, I really cannot . . . honestly . . . don't start that again, dear. No, don't . . . Em . . . I can't."

"Don't whine, Custis. It is not becoming in a man."

"Oh, shit."

"I will not take you a mile out of your way, darlin'," she said happily. "Not one single li'l old mile. Now be quiet while I finish doing you. But hurry, will you, please? We don't want to be late getting on the road this morning."

"Look, I am sorry. I really am. But . . . damn, that feels good, what you're doin' down there . . . but I got to tell you, girl, it doesn't matter how good you are or how much you please me, I simply cannot take you with me on that prison wagon. I'm sorry, kid, but there is just no damned way I can do that. None."

Chapter 5

"Now aren't you glad I came along?" Emily asked, sitting prim and proper on the far side of the driving bench. For the first three days of their journey, Emily had been a sex-craved little tigress. Now that they were coming close to her home territory, she was the prissy little schoolmarm; butter wouldn't melt in her mouth, much less a hard cock. Why, she would surely be shocked to the point of fainting had someone even mentioned that piece of male anatomy.

Longarm looked at the girl and shook his head. She was quite something, this Miss Emily. And the truth was that he enjoyed her almighty well. He could enjoy her almost to the point of settling down and staying with just one woman for the rest of his days, with just her.

Almost, that is. But he was tempted. He actually was. He wondered if she knew the depth of his feeling for her, already strong and still growing. He opened his mouth to say something about that. Not to come right out and make any declaration, mind. But to sort of sneak up sideways toward the subject. "D'you, uh, d'you know . . ."

"Oh, darlin', we're awful close now, awful close. I remember . . . I just remember *every*thing here. Over there in that swale there's a tangle of wild blackberries where I used to sneak off when I was little. Oh, they just tasted *so* good. And over there in that field I turned my ankle once and thought it was broken and my daddy picked me up and carried me all the way up to the house. He never stopped to rest nor set me down, just carried me all the way and me bawling and running snot and being a baby about things, but it wasn't broken after all and my mama bound it up nice and tight and made me stay off it for three days and after that it was tender but nothing worse than that and . . . ooo! Custis, look! Up there. You can see the top of the roof there. Can't you see it, darlin'? Can't you?"

He had to smile at her enthusiasm. Lordy, she was one pretty little bit of a thing. There were times when he actually forgot how old she was and started thinking of her as the little girl she played on stage. And then there were other times when the horny imp came out and all he wanted was to crawl inside her naked body and never come out again.

Longarm snapped upright, amazed at himself. Had he just had a thought that included the idea of *never* letting go of this one? That was not . . . well, it was not like him. Really.

"Are you all right, darlin'?" she asked.

"Yes, of course. Why d'you ask?"

"Because all of a sudden you looked almost . . . scared, that's why."

"Just startled a little. I was thinking." He grinned and added, "That's such a rare thing, I don't wonder that you would find it surprisin'."

"You're sure you are all right now?"

"Yes, Emily, I'm sure. But I thank you for askin'."

"Oh. Custis. Look there." She was practically bounc-

24

ing up and down on the seat of the prison wagon. "That's the foot of our drive. That's the path up to the house. You can stop right there and let me out, darlin'. I can walk the rest of the way."

"There's no need for that, Em. I can drive you—"

"Now, Custis, we have been over and over this, and this is the way I want to do it. I don't mind a little walk, and it would be awkward for my folks to see me with a fine gentleman such as yourself."

"But they don't need to know that . . ."

She reached up and laid a fingertip across his lips. "Hush now, darlin'. I know my parents and I know how to handle this. And that does not include having you with me."

"If you say so," he grumbled, the words half under his breath. The truth was that his feelings were hurt.

"I do say so. If you knew my parents, you would understand."

"And that is the point, Em. I would kinda like to meet your folks. That'd give me a better understanding of you."

"Later, darlin'. There is time enough for that sort of thing later."

He was not sure how to take that. As encouragement? Or a brush-off. It could be either one. Dammit.

"Ooo, ooo! Stop here, Custis. Right here. Oh, darlin', I am so excited."

Before he could jump down to help her, Emily leaped off the driving box and hit the ground with her skirts flying in a most unladylike manner. She was beaming with excitement.

"Oh, darlin', I am so happy. Thank you for bringing me. And don't forget. When you get back, just stop right here. I'll be watching that day. I'll see you and come running."

"What if you don't see me?"

"I will," she said happily, the source of that joy in the little house on top of the hill where they now were.

Emily practically lunged at the wagon to retrieve her suitcase.

"That's awful heavy, Em. Won't you let me—"

"Not another word, Custis. We have been through this over and over. I can manage. Now you go on and do your deputy thing. I will be here ready to return to Denver when you get back."

Longarm sighed. "Aren't you going to give me a good-bye kiss at the least?"

"Certainly not. Someone might see."

Longarm looked around. He had not seen another human being in the past eight or nine miles. And damned few animals. This was crop-farming country.

"Gracious, darlin', I drained that sweet old cock of yours twice this morning before we stepped out in public. That will just have to hold you until you get back." She giggled. "In fact, it is probably a good idea for you to think about it. It will make sure you come back for me."

"There's no question about that, sweet thing."

"Oh, I know how you men are. You will have forgotten about me before this wagon gets out of sight." She ducked under the horses' noses and came around to his side of the rig, stopping beside the driving box.

From a distance, it would have looked like she was simply thanking the person who had given her a ride out to her folks' place. Up close, however . . . the damn girl laid her hand on Longarm's thigh and felt of his pecker, squeezing and kneading it like a piece of dough. Rising dough.

"Damn you."

Emily laughed, her eyes bright and her curls bouncing. Without another word, she turned and began running up the hill toward her parents' house.

Longarm shook his head. She was one helluva girl that Emily.

Then he shook out the driving lines and put the team into motion. According to Emily, he was within a few hours of Edwardsville.

It was time to get down to business.

Chapter 6

Edwardsville, D.T., was no bigger than it had to be. And not so big as it ought to be. It had a stone courthouse, but things went downhill from there. The few buildings were sun-bleached and wind-blasted. It was a place for mules and dirt farmers. Longarm felt out of place.

A sleepy-eyed clerk in the courthouse told him the sheriff's office was in the basement. "But don't bother looking for him now. He's gone over to Harper's to see about a robbery there. And don't bother asking me when he'll be back, for I wouldn't know."

"All right, thanks." Longarm went back outside and drove the wagon around to the back of the courthouse. He parked it there, then led the team down the street to the blacksmith's. A sign posted there offered used farm equipment for sale. It also advertised livery services.

"I'd like to put these animals up for the night," he told the boy in his teens who was in charge.

"Fifty cents apiece, sir. He, uh, he likes to be paid in advance." The boy sounded worried that Longarm would think his honesty was doubted by the request for payment in advance.

"That's fine, son." Longarm dug a silver dollar out of

his pocket and handed it across. He could ask for a receipt when he picked up the horses, he figured. By then the smith should be back to date and sign it. Henry would want the receipt or he would balk at including the item on Longarm's expense voucher.

"I'll take care of them for you, sir. Don't you worry about that."

"I trust that you will. Tell me, where can a visitor get a meal around here?"

"There's the saloon out at the end of town. They serve food there. Or, um, that's what I've heard."

Longarm grinned. It was clear the boy had been known to slip inside the establishment at least once in the past. It was equally clear that he was not supposed to be there.

"The better place," the kid went on, "is Miss Hilda's. It isn't a proper café really. It's a boardinghouse, but she serves meals on her side porch if there's extra. She pretty much always cooks extra. Just in case."

"And that would be . . . ?"

"On the other side of the general store, then the next street over. It's a two-story house. The only one in town. You aren't likely to miss it."

"No, I reckon I can find it if it's the only one."

"Yes, sir."

"Thank you, son." Longarm pulled a dime out and offered it to the boy.

"What's that for, sir?"

"It's a tip. For being so helpful."

The kid shook his head and refused to reach out for the money. "I haven't done anything but what's right, sir. You don't have to pay me for that."

"Good Lord! An honest youngster. And a decent one. Who'd of ever thought it."

"Sir?"

"Never mind. You're sure about the money?"

30

"Yes, sir, but thank you."

Longarm left the horses in the boy's care and walked back the way he had just come. He found the general store easily enough. It occupied most of a rather ill-defined city block, the rest of that block grown up in weeds and littered with trash. It seemed that Edwardsville had planned for more in the way of growth than ever came to it, for a good half the building lots were vacant.

There were, however, a number of streets laid out running more or less parallel with at least four cross streets intersecting the primary east-west streets. He found Hilda's two-story boardinghouse with ease and walked up onto the porch.

There was a bell pull beside the front door. He tugged it, and a brief chime sounded somewhere inside. A moment later a woman came to the door. A huge woman. Or a small mountain. He was not sure how she ought to be categorized.

Longarm almost forgot to take his hat off, he was so amazed by her appearance. Miss Hilda was . . . immense. Taller than Longarm and with hips that were a good ax-handle broad. Hair piled in an unruly bun. Face heat-reddened. A waist Longarm doubted he could reach around with both arms . . . yet on her huge frame managing to look almost small. And tits. Tits most women would need a wheelbarrow to carry.

Make that a pair of wheelbarrows.

Longarm gaped.

He was being rude. He knew it. He just could not damned well help himself.

"Yes? What is it? Speak up, dammit, you're the one rang the bell, not me."

"I, uh, that is . . ."

"Are you hungry? Do you want a room?"

It occurred to Longarm that he was unlikely to get

31

his prisoner this afternoon, what with the sheriff being away. And anyway, it was only fair to give Emily some time to visit her parents before he picked her up for the trip back to Denver.

"I am hungry, yes. And I do need a room, please."

"Huh. Pretty little thing, aren't you? And you got manners too. I like you," Hilda said.

Longarm blinked. It was bad enough being called pretty. But *little*? "I, uh, thank you."

"Well don't just stand there. Come inside. You got no luggage?"

"I have a bag. I left it in my wagon. I'll bring it over later."

The woman grunted. "All right then. Are you hungry now? My regulars has already had lunch, but there's leftovers."

"Whatever you have will be fine."

"Then come in. We'll see if we can't put some meat on those bones." Hilda pushed the screen door open and beckoned for him to enter. "My name is Pettijohn, by the way. The Widow Pettijohn."

Longarm introduced himself.

"And what business brings you this way, Mr. Long? You say you have a wagon? Would you be selling anything I'd be interested in?"

Longarm laughed and told the woman who and what he was.

"Here for that Handley fella, you say. Now I will tell you how you can make yourself popular around here, Marshal Long. You can turn that man loose on the street. I can tell you true, before he could reach the edge of town in any direction, Jack Handley would be torn limb from limb. It would be like a pack of wolves bringing down a bull moose, it would. Why, the very idea of what he did! He should have his balls ripped off, Marshal Long. It would be doing all womankind a favor if someone was to do exactly that."

"I don't think that punishment is permitted by the courts."

"Maybe not, but it ought to be."

"Yes, ma'am."

She led him through the parlor and onto a pleasantly shaded side porch where there was a table long enough to seat a dozen diners without any one of them being crowded for elbow room. "You set here, Marshal Long. Do you like roast buffalo with gravy and taters and dried apple pie for after?"

"You bet I do."

"Then you're in luck. Set right down and let me take care of you, you pretty little thing."

Longarm was not sure why, but he was beginning to feel like a fly with its feet stuck to a strip of flypaper.

But damn, that woman could cook!

Chapter 7

The saloon at the edge of town, the place that also served meals, was a rat hole. No wonder that boy at the blacksmith's shop had suggested Hilda Pettijohn instead. Longarm would not have wanted to put anything into his mouth if it came from Sy's Salune—which was what a small sign over the door proclaimed the place to be.

One look inside the place was bad enough. Worse was actually stepping through the door and smelling the stench of old puke and sun-cured sweat. Hell, he wouldn't want even the rim of a whiskey bottle to touch his lips in there. And this from a man who had consumed more than his fair share of unidentifiable foods and beverages in Indian lodges across much of the West. He turned right around and walked over to the general store.

"D'you have rye whiskey here?"

"Of course, but you have to buy the whole bottle. I don't sell drinks one at a time."

"It's the bottle I'm wanting, friend," Longarm told the scrawny clerk.

"Rye be all right for you? Or I have some bourbon straight from Kentucky."

"Rye is perfect."

The clerk pulled a stepladder along the wall behind the counter so he could get one of the bottles down from the shelving. Longarm recognized the label. It was Pennsylvania distilled and very good.

"That will be two dollars, mister. Is there anything else you need?"

"Cheroots if you have them, or a good panatela."

The clerk set an array of five cigar boxes on the counter and opened them for his customer to examine. There were some cheroots, two brands that Longarm had not encountered before. He plucked one of each out of the cedarwood boxes and smelled of them before making his selection. "I'll take these, please."

"How many would you like?"

"I'll take the box." There were some advantages to traveling in a wagon instead of living out of his Gladstone bag alone. He had space enough to drag along cigars by the case if he wanted.

"Oh, my. Yes, that is fine."

"That will be all then."

"Three dollars and a half," the clerk said, sounding more than a little apologetic . . . and like he expected the stranger to back out of the sale. Longarm guessed that most of the folks around here were not overly burdened with cash money.

"Would you like me to wrap those for you?"

"That'd be fine, thanks." Longarm waited for the few moments it took for the gent to wrap his purchases in heavy brown paper and tie the small bundle with string. He paid with cash—no receipt necessary for this nonvoucher purchase—and touched the brim of his hat to the store owner.

A visit to the courthouse disclosed no sheriff and no information about when that worthy gentleman might return from the crossroads community at Harper's store. Longarm was not sure where Harper's was, but Emily had mentioned it several times. Apparently, it was a country store where her parents sometimes shopped, it being closer for them than the drive all the way to Edwardsville.

He left the courthouse and went around back to the prison wagon, where he retrieved his gear and carried it back to the boardinghouse.

"Mr. Long. You're back early."

"Yes, ma'am, Miz Pettijohn. The sheriff isn't in and I can't accomplish much until he gets back."

"Let me show you to your room then."

"I'd appreciate it."

"But please. Call me Hilda."

"Yes, ma'am. Uh, I mean—"

"It's all right. Whatever is comfortable for you. Down the hall here. Right beside the kitchen is where you will sleep." She came to the appropriate door and pushed it open. "If you want to smoke, do it on the porch, please. Otherwise the odor gets into the curtains."

"Yes, ma'am."

"And I am not one to pry nor do I judge, but I see that is a bottle that is wrapped up in that bundle there. I have nothing against a drink now and then. In fact, I enjoy a little whiskey myself at times. Feel free to help yourself to the glasses you will find in the kitchen. And you can take the bottle with you to the porch if you like. I do not mind if a bottle is seen on my property. I am not one to worry about what the neighbors think."

"Why, thank you, ma'am. Uh, Hilda, I mean." It was mildly unnerving to be standing next to this huge, thick-bodied female creature and be looking *up* at her. But she seemed nice enough and she was no damned prude. As landladies went, Hilda was not so bad.

37

"Would you like me to bring you a glass, Mr. Long?"

"Sure, Hilda. That'd be nice of you. You say you like a little drink now and then your own self?"

"Yes, I do."

"Then why don't you bring two glasses. I'll meet you on the porch an' we can pass a little time there."

"That we can do, Mr. Long. That we can do."

Chapter 8

It was nice sitting on the porch with a glass and a bottle, but the sun was sinking fast and he was not accomplishing a damn thing by being there. Hilda had gone back inside long since. He could hear the occasional clash of dishware and could constantly smell the rich, marvelous scents that were coming out of her kitchen as she prepared dinner for her boarders.

Longarm finished his drink and dipped into his vest pocket for the bulbous Ingersol he carried there. It was a railroad-quality timepiece, as reliable as a rock and damn near as rugged as one too. An outdoorsman's habit made him look at the time, then tilt his head and squint at the sun to verify that the mechanical contrivance was indeed matching the creator's order of things.

Yeah, it was past five o'clock by both measures. Longarm stood, stretched, and decided to wander over to the courthouse before the clerk went home for the day. It could be the man had news of the sheriff. For that matter, the sheriff might be back by now.

It was too late to start back with Handley now even if he received custody of the man, but at least they could get the paperwork out of the way. God, but he hated paperwork.

Longarm stepped down into the street and headed out at a brisk walk. It took only a few minutes to reach the courthouse, which was still open. There was a young couple in the clerk's office when Longarm got there. The lady was red-cheeked and round. Doubly so. She was plump, but she was also pregnant. The boy beside her was tall and gangly and intense.

The young fellow probably never in his life had heard a shot fired in anger nor seen a man cut down in his prime. Longarm looked at the two of them and wished for them that neither ever would be exposed to the cruel violence that he so constantly encountered in his line of work.

There were times when Longarm thought of himself as a garbage collector. The job was necessary, but it did nothing to enrich society, merely cleaned out the crap that sank to the bottom and chucked it away.

This young couple here, they could add something to the world. Children who might someday devise ways to make the world a better place. At the least they would be contributing food for folks to eat. Looking at them, Longarm felt a wave of loneliness sweep over him like a cold wave.

And yet he was proud of what he did and he did it well, he . . . He paused and grinned. He'd had about a drink and a half too much, that was what he'd done.

The young couple finished their business with the clerk. Longarm snatched his hat off out of respect for the young lady and stepped aside to let them pass. The boy seemed proud. He held himself upright and awkward as he escorted her out.

"Hello again," the clerk said as Longarm approached the counter.

"Howdy. The sheriff back yet?"

The man shook his head. "Sorry. I haven't seen him nor heard a peep out of him. Do you absolutely have to see him this evening?"

"No, not really. It can wait until morning. I do wonder, though, when the sheriff is out of town like this, does he have a deputy who takes care of feeding his prisoners?"

"Nope, there's no one else. Just the sheriff."

"And the prisoners?"

"Truth is, we don't often have any. And for that matter, the sheriff isn't often away from the town. If he's going to drive around to the other communities, which he tries to do at least once every month, he generally picks a time when the jail is empty. I suppose in a pinch his wife could feed them for him."

"I see. Thank you."

"Is there anything else?"

"No, the business I have will have to be with the sheriff."

"In that case, I'll be closing up and going home." The clerk smiled. "Got to see what sort of burnt offering my missus puts on the table tonight. She's a fine woman, my wife. Pillar of the community. Sings in the choir every week. Never utters a cross word. But Lordy, I wish we could afford to hire a cook."

Longarm laughed. As he was supposed to, of course. But he could not help wondering if there was a germ of truth hidden in there, the poor son of a bitch. Deadly dull work. Wife who couldn't cook. Maybe being a lawman wasn't so rotten after all.

"Thank you, sir. I'll, uh, check with you again tomorrow."

"I'll be here."

And that, Longarm thought, was the final truth that made him appreciate what he did for his livelihood. A man like this county clerk indeed would be here tomorrow and tomorrow's tomorrow and all the days after that.

What a dreary damned prospect. It could be that Custis Long did not have it so awfully bad after all.

He went outside and stood in the slanting light of late afternoon. After a few minutes, he started back to the boardinghouse. Supper should be ready soon.

Chapter 9

After supper, Longarm went out onto the porch for a smoke. There were only two other boarders staying at Hilda Pettijohn's place. Both of them came onto the porch too, but both put their caps on once they set foot out the door.

"Where're you gents off to?" Longarm asked, fairly sure he already knew the answer to that judging by the eager tension in the men's bodies. His guess was that the crappy, rundown saloon at the edge of town had at least one buxom farm lass doing business there at night.

"We're going to, um, stretch our legs. A little," the one fellow said.

"That's right," the other one chimed in. "Stretch our legs, y'see."

"Right." Longarm nodded sagely, as if the two had said something important. Or anyway, like he believed them. Which he did not. "Have a pleasant evening then."

The men stepped down off the porch and then the second man, who had a faint accent that Longarm could not quite place, turned and said, "You could come along if you like."

43

Longarm smiled. Quite genuinely. It was a mighty kind offer and he truly appreciated it. "Thank you, sir, but for the moment I'm content enough sitting in this rocking chair enjoying the evening air and a cigar. Perhaps I'll run into you later."

"Yeah. Later then."

The two gents hurried on their way. Wanting to be toward the front of the line when the "gents" of Edwardsville lined up to have a crack at the local whore? Longarm shuddered. The prospect of having so many men and so few sporting gals as was likely found in this small town . . . it would be like using a public toilet; a man would want to take care about what he got on himself.

Longarm finished his smoke and thought about going inside, maybe inviting Hilda to have another drink with him. It was not a good idea at the moment, though. He could hear the clatter and clash of dishware coming from the back of the house. Hilda was washing the supper dishes. And Custis Long had no intention whatsoever of being roped into that little domestic chore.

Instead, he ambled down the street.

Without any particular destination in mind, he found himself approaching the courthouse, and he wondered about the prisoner who was supposed to be in there. After all, he had yet to lay eyes on the man.

The sheriff's office and jail were in the basement of the courthouse building. A set of steps at the back of the building led down to the basement level without the need to enter the courthouse itself. Longarm went down and tried the door.

"It's locked," a voice called from inside, giving Longarm information that he'd already discovered without that assistance. "The sheriff's gone. I have no idea when he'll be back."

"Are you the deputy?" Longarm responded although he already knew the answer to that.

"I'm the prisoner."

"What's you name?"

"John H. Handley. What's yours?"

"Custis Long. How are you doing in there?"

"Thirsty. Hungry. Scared. Horny. Apart from those things, though, I'm doing just fine, thank you."

Longarm chuckled. Jack Handley might be a real son of a bitch, but the man had a sense of humor about it all. Longarm liked that.

"You haven't eaten this evening?"

"Not since breakfast," Handley answered.

"I'd say you have a right to be hungry then."

"And I'd say that you are right, Mr. Long."

"That's Deputy Long, actually. I've come to take you back to Colorado for trial there."

"Just my luck. I finally meet a man who understands me and it turns out that he understands me all too well."

"Ain't that just the way of the world," Longarm observed. "Is there a way to get in here?"

"Sure is," Handley called back. "The sheriff leaves a key tucked in a niche between the foundation stones right where you're standing. It's about shoulder high to a normal-sized fellow and just to the right of the door."

"He leaves a key?" Longarm asked while he was busy feeling around between the stones. He was not at all certain that Handley wasn't having him on, but he wanted to look anyway.

"He kept losing them. Finally the blacksmith, the man who had to make all the replacement keys, got tired of filing new ones. He made the sheriff promise to hide one. Said he wasn't going to make any new ones after that, that the sheriff would have to go over to Cory if he wanted any more keys made. Said it was too much work to be worth the bother."

"Ah. Found it," Longarm said, extracting the key from its hiding place.

"Are you coming inside?"

"In a minute, I am, yes."

"Do you want me to wait here for you?" Handley asked.

"If you feel like it," Longarm said, then hurried back to Hilda's place. He figured it was reasonable enough for the Justice Department to pay for a dinner even though the prisoner was not technically in their custody yet. Longarm just purely hated the idea of a man having to go hungry through no fault of his own, even if he was a rapist and a murderer like this John H. Handley.

Besides, Longarm sort of liked the man, what little he had heard of him. So far.

For fifty cents, Hilda packed a sumptuous dinner of fried pork, pole beans, cornbread, and stewed apples, putting it all into a basket along with a napkin, butter knife, and spoon. Both of those last items Longarm intended to check on when he left the jail later, to make sure they did not stay behind with Handley. Longarm did not know much about this prisoner, but he knew prisoners in general. And either a dull knife or spoon handle can be turned into a jim-dandy weapon with a little rubbing against rough stone to create a blade.

He carried the basket back to the jail and let himself in with the sheriff's key, then replaced the key where it belonged. He did wonder, though, how many others around Edwardsville knew about that key if a traveling man like Handley did.

Once inside, he had to find and light a lantern

against the gathering darkness. When he did that he got a mild surprise.

John Handley certainly did not *look* like a murderer and a rapist.

The man looked like, well, he looked pretty much like a happy Christmas elf. He was about five feet tall and another five around his girth. Or anyway, that was the impression he gave. Moreover, the round little fellow had a shiny bald dome, a fluffy snow-white beard, and a thin fringe of white around his head.

Handley grinned when he saw Longarm's reaction.

"It's gonna be like traveling with St. Nicholas," Longarm mumbled, which brought a roar of laughter from Handley.

"My, oh, my," Handley returned. "Think of the disappointment you will cause among children all the way from here back to . . . where is it that we will be going, anyway?"

"Manitou," Longarm told him.

"Ah, yes. That little affair . . . no, let me rephrase that . . . that little problem with Ed Marsh, I should assume."

"Problem?" Longarm asked as he parceled out the goodies in the basket and handed them through the bars. He did not know where there was a key so he could open the door and hand the whole basket in. Although Jack Handley probably knew if Longarm only cared to ask him.

"I shot and killed the man," Handley said without changing expression. He arranged the plate and food carefully on his bunk and perched beside it, then bowed his head, his lips moving presumably in prayer. It was not a gesture Longarm generally saw in his prisoners.

"You admit to it," Longarm said.

"Certainly I do. I did it. No doubt about it." Handley

used the knife and spoon to laboriously saw a chink of pork off a juicy chop.

"Be easier to pick that up and gnaw on it," Longarm observed.

"Without question," Handley agreed. He began to tear another bite-sized piece off with the dull knife.

"Well?" Longarm asked when Handley offered no more explanation than the fact that he had indeed murdered that postal clerk.

"Well, what?"

"Is that all you intend to say about the murder?"

"What murder?"

"Ed whatshisname's murder," Longarm said.

"There was no murder, Deputy. There was a killing, yes. I did that in full view of a room full of people, but that killing was pure self-defense. It was no murder."

"I thought . . ."

"Of course you did. You probably also think I sodomized that girl here in Dakota Territory."

"You were convicted of it."

"So I was," Handley said calmly.

"And . . . ?"

Handley laid down his knife and spoon and patiently said, "The young lady in question, Long, was the one who approached me. I stopped at her family's farm to ask a drink for myself and for my horse. Afterward, I asked if I could pull around to the side of their barn and rest there in the shade for a little while. The father said that I could.

"The girl came to me. She said if I would give her a dollar she would suck my dick. It seemed a reasonable arrangement, a little extra cash for her, a little innocent pleasure for me. I agreed. I paid her the dollar. I opened my fly and she got on her knees in the driving box of my wagon.

"The two of us were in that posture, the girl with her

mouth on my member, when her father came around the corner of the barn and caught us. I tried to explain. That was a waste of breath. So . . . here I am."

"I see." Longarm chewed on the inside of his cheek for a moment, then asked, "Had you paid her the dollar?"

Handley looked puzzled. "Why would you ask a thing like that?"

Longarm shrugged.

"As it happened," Handley said, "yes, I had. It is customary for a soiled dove to collect payment in advance, or at least that has been my experience in the past."

"It's usual, yes," Longarm agreed.

Handley went back to his supper. When he was done with it, he handed the empty plates—and the knife and spoon—out to Longarm, who replaced it all in Hilda's basket ready to carry back to the boardinghouse.

He rather suspected he would have a pleasant drive back to Colorado what with both Emily Balcolm and Jack Handley for company along the way.

Chapter 10

"Sheriff!" The man skidded to a halt in the middle of the room. "Dammit, where's the sheriff?"

Longarm looked at the obviously very distressed farmer and said, "He's out at . . . hell, I don't remember where he's gone."

"He had to go over to Harper's store," Handley put in from behind his jail bars. "He's been gone all day."

"Well they need him over at Sy's."

"That would be the local watering hole," Handley put in.

"Yes, I remember. The saloon." Longarm returned his attention to the farmer who had just come bursting into the jail. "What's the problem over there, friend?"

"Jimmy Dryden has a knife and he's threatening to gut Tom Corliss."

"Do you think he's serious?"

"Damn if I know, mister, but he's drunk enough that I'd believe most anything."

Longarm sighed. It had been such a pleasant evening. Right up until now. "All right. I'll come see what I can do."

"Who're you?"

"U.S. deputy marshal."

"Oh. Well . . . all right. But Jimmy, he might not care. He's mad enough an' drunk enough he likely won't give a shit who you are."

"That's all right, friend. I don't much give a shit who he is either, not when it comes to keeping the peace."

"Mister, you ain't seen Jimmy yet. He's big an' he's mean an' he has an awful big knife."

"Then let's go fetch him here. He can keep Mr. Handley company tonight."

"Yes, sir." The farmer turned and ran outside. Longarm paused long enough to pick up his hat. "I'll be back."

"That would be the optimistic point of view," Handley said as Longarm was on his way out.

He broke into a run once he reached the street, but slowed short of Sy's Salune. Whatever was going on in there, they were being mighty quiet about it. And Longarm's experience was that once a saloon grew silent there was some very serious stuff going on.

The farmer who had brought the bad news hung back and quickly disappeared completely, apparently having pressing business elsewhere that needed tending to. That was all right. He had done his best. He'd reported the problem. The rest was up to Longarm.

Inside the saloon, the scene was like a motionless tableau in the middle of a melodrama. Except there was no blushing maiden of the sort Emily might play. Instead, there was a plump whore sitting on the floor weeping. Two men, customers probably, were kneeling beside another man whose left forearm was bleeding heavily. One of the kneeling men was tying a wet and none-too-clean bar towel around the wound.

And standing facing all four of them was a human mountain. He was wearing worn and tattered bib overalls like nearly every other male in or around Edwardsville, but his must have been sewn up special for him. By a tentmaker.

The man was half a head taller than Longarm and probably outweighed him by a hundred fifty pounds. A lot of that was fat, but certainly not all of it.

He had a dark, full beard and his hair looked like it had not been combed nor curried since the last time he cut it.

Most interesting of all was the slim, pointed blade of the Arkansas pigsticker he held in his right hand. Everything else about the man might be unkempt and disheveled, but the knife looked like he kept it sharp and oiled.

The huge man heard Longarm come in. He turned and growled. If he wanted to imitate a bear, he could do a pretty good job of it with a growl like that. "Get out."

Longarm flipped his wallet open to display his badge and said, "I'm a United States deputy marshal. And you, I presume, would be Jimmy Dryden."

"I don't much give a shit who you think you are. Get outa here, bub. Right now."

Longarm hooked his thumbs behind his belt buckle. He rather hoped Dryden would notice that the gesture, common enough in any case, put his hand only a few inches from the worn butt of his Colt .44-.40.

"You are drunk and you are causing a public disturbance. That is against your town ordinances, Dryden. I am gonna walk you over to the jail so's you can sleep off the liquor. The sheriff will see to the rest of it with you when he gets back."

"Go fuck yourself."

Longarm smiled calmly. "I have to admit that it would be damned convenient if I could figure out how to do that. In the meantime, I'll just have to make do with women."

"Huh?"

"Never mind. The concept is probably too deep for a man like you t' grasp," Longarm said.

"What the hell is that s'pose to mean?"

"The man just called you stupid, Jimmy, and you're too damn dumb to even know it," the fellow with the bleeding arm said.

Longarm winced. There could have been better times for him to put his two cents worth in. And better things he could've said when he did.

"You shut your damn pie hole, Tom. Soon as I'm done with Mr. Fancy Pants here, I'm gonna shut you up for good, d'you hear me?"

Tom Corliss blanched and very quickly shut his pie hole, suddenly clamping his mouth tightly closed after opening it as if to say something more.

Jimmy Dryden turned to face Longarm and waved the point of the Arkansas toothpick at him. "You better git now," he warned.

"I don't think so, Jimmy. Now I want you to put the knife down. Just lay it on the bar there. They'll keep it safe for you until you sober up. No one is gonna try to take it away from you. We just want you to sober up before you mess with it again. After all, I'm sure you don't want to hurt anyone."

"Bull *shit,* I don't!"

Dryden raised the knife and charged directly at Longarm.

"Well, hell," Longarm mumbled.

The big Colt flashed in his hand. Flame spit out of the muzzle and smoke filled the low-ceilinged room.

Longarm's slug ripped through Dryden's throat and passed on through, severing his vertebrae slightly below the skull.

Blood flew in a pink and red halo behind him and his head, no longer supported by what remained of his neck, flopped over at an obscene angle.

Jimmy Dryden was dead long before his body hit the straw-covered saloon floor.

"Jesus!" someone breathed.

Longarm said, "Shit. I didn't wanta have to do that."

"I never seen . . . never seen . . ." The fellow with the bar towel, presumably Sy, spun around and puked into a spittoon. Or at least onto it, the capacity of the brass receptacle falling well short of being able to hold all the vomit.

The whore was screaming and the men were pale. All of them were obviously shocked by the sudden violence. It was not what these farmers were accustomed to.

Longarm grunted and shucked the empty cartridge case out of his Colt, then slipped a fresh round into that chamber.

"Saves the county the cost of feeding him until his trial," he said to no one in particular.

Then he turned and walked out into the fresh air of evening.

"Shit," he grumbled aloud when he was halfway back to the jail. "Well, just . . . shit!"

Chapter 11

"What's wrong, Marshal? You look . . . I don't know. Weary, I suppose," Handley said when Longarm returned to the jail. "I heard a gunshot. Was it yours?"

Longarm nodded, then almost reluctantly filled his sympathetic prisoner in on the death of Jimmy Dryden.

"You did what had to be done to protect others, but this shooting is really bothering you, isn't it?"

"Yeah," Longarm admitted. "Maybe it is. God knows why. I've killed men before. Too damned many of them. I just didn't want to . . . oh, never mind. It doesn't matter. Nothing matters."

"If there is anything I can do to help, Marshal . . ."

Longarm gave the rotund little prisoner a hard look, then decided that Jack Handley was not being facetious. He meant it. Longarm's expression softened a little. "Thanks. But never mind. I'll get over it." He retrieved Hilda Pettijohn's basket from on top of the sheriff's desk where he had set it earlier, then let himself out and locked the jail door behind him.

Hilda was in the kitchen, still cleaning up after supper and preparing some of the foods she would cook come morning. She took one look at Longarm and asked, "What is wrong? Your face is gray. Are you sick?"

"No. I'm fine."

"You are a liar too then. Anyone can see that you are troubled."

"It's nothing. I'll get over it. Where's the rest of that bottle you and me were enjoying this afternoon?"

Hilda fetched the whiskey bottle out of a cupboard and handed it to Longarm. If she had any rules about guests drinking in their rooms at night, she did not say anything about that now.

"G'night, Hilda."

She hesitated for a moment, then nodded and said, "Good night then."

Longarm went to his room and slumped down onto the edge of the bed.

He pulled the cork out of the bottle and tossed it away, then raised the bottle to his mouth.

Drowning. He was drowning. No air. He couldn't breathe!

Longarm tried to sit upright, only to find he was blanketed by some warm, moist, pillowy soft weight that was smothering him.

He wasn't dreaming. He thought he had been, but not now.

And he was not drowning.

But he was damn sure suffocating.

He turned his head and tried to squirm out from under the weight that was pressing down on his chest and making it so hard for him to breathe.

"Careful now." The voice came to him slightly muffled but very close by. "Am I too heavy? I'm sorry, dear."

Mrs. Pettijohn. Good God! She was . . . the woman was naked. Those weren't pillows, they were her tits.

And they did indeed threaten to suffocate him as she lay atop his lean body.

The bottle . . . Longarm's head spun. He remembered finishing the bottle. Then he wasn't sure. Passed out maybe. And now this.

"What you need, dear, is to relieve some of the harshness that is in you. You need to let go of your cares for a few minutes. I can help you. Now close your eyes. That's right. Just lie back and relax. Don't think about a thing except for what you feel. Here. And here."

He damn near came upright again at the unexpected tugging at him. But then . . .

He must have gotten an erection in his sleep although he hadn't been aware of it. Must have, though, because now he could certainly feel it. Could feel his cock enveloped in warmth. Moist, smooth, warm. It wrapped around him. Drew him in and slowly let him out again. The woman's touch was so soft and subtle that it actually took him a moment to realize that he was being drawn inside big Hilda Pettijohn's mouth.

Despite his size, she was able to take all of him. Without the scrape of teeth on tender flesh too. Longarm needed another few disoriented moments to comprehend that Hilda did not have any teeth in her mouth. She must have taken them out and left them somewhere.

Oh, but he could feel her gums and tongue . . . and throat.

She moved very slowly up and down on his shaft, and Longarm's responses grew right along with his awareness of what the woman was doing to him.

Without warning, entirely unexpected, he felt that magical, mystical, marvelous gathering of fullness deep in his balls and the flooding release of semen flowing sweet and tingling through the length of his cock to spill out into the warm orifice of Mrs. Pettijohn's mouth.

Longarm groaned. And went limp.

Collapsed was more like it. He felt drained. But it was not only his juice that was drained away. The dark and ugly despair that had been tormenting him was gone as well, washed away by the sweet flood of jism.

"There, dear. Go back to sleep now."

The weight was lifted from his chest—but more importantly, the bleakness was lifted from his soul—and she was gone.

After a few moments, Longarm was not entirely sure she had ever been there. He might well have dreamed the whole thing.

Except there was a slippery wetness at his crotch where some fluid continued to leak out of him.

It was all right regardless. Whatever happened here, or whatever he imagined happened here, he felt relaxed now and at peace.

Longarm closed his eyes and dropped into a deep, restful sleep.

Chapter 12

Longarm felt like shit. His head throbbed and his tongue was coated with fur and direct sunshine might very well blind him. But he was in a good humor despite all that. This was a new day and all was right with the world. He planted his hat onto his head—carefully—and stepped out onto the street, wincing only a little bit at the sharp bite of daylight.

"Good morning, Marshal," Jack Handley called out when Longarm let himself into the sheriff's office. "Sheriff Dwight isn't back yet. Sorry."

Longarm was in such a good mood this morning that he didn't even care. "I don't suppose anyone brought you breakfast."

"No."

"All right. Wait there. I'll be right back." He returned to the boardinghouse—where Hilda Pettijohn acted like the night's activities never happened; and for that matter Longarm would not have sworn that they were not a dream—and bought another basket of grub, courtesy of the United States government.

Back at the jail again, he fed Handley and gave a squint at the nearly full bucket under the jail cell bunk.

61

The thing needed emptying. Badly. But Longarm did not have a key to get the door open. The task would just have to wait until the sheriff returned.

Longarm was just packing up the dirty dishware to return to Hilda when the jail door swung open and a tall man with gray hair and more than his fair share of belly came in.

"Who the hell are you and what are you doing in my jail?"

"Sheriff, let me introduce the man who's come to take me to my hanging," said Handley. "This is Deputy Marshal Custis Long."

"Oh. Shit. And I thought I was seeing history made, the first time anybody ever broke *into* jail." Dwight smiled and extended his hand. "Call me Tom."

"I'm Longarm," he said, glad to accept the handshake.

"Longarm," Dwight repeated. "When you said your name is Long, I thought maybe you were the one they call that."

"They?"

"Sy Bitterman. He grabbed me on my way into town and started in on me about who's to pay for a certain burying."

"Oh, yes. That. Sorry, Sheriff. I didn't come here to cause you any problems."

Dwight shrugged. "Jimmy has been pushing his luck for a long time. Just his poor fortune to come up against someone who doesn't have to worry about what the voters might think. That can free a man to do what needs doing."

"It can also free a man to run roughshod if there's no reins to hold him in," Longarm said.

"That's true. In any case, Jimmy has been a problem for a long while. His luck finally ran out."

"So who will pay for the burying?" Longarm asked.

"Oh, we'll put it on the county's account. Might as

well. It seems a whole lot of our resources will be going for burials this quarter anyway."

Longarm raised an eyebrow.

"This is a nice, quiet county, Longarm. We never have troubles here, not violent ones anyway. At least we never used to."

"And now?"

"Down at Harper's Store. Two people dead. Harper himself and his old lady too. Not just killed. Butchered. Robbed, of course. The folks . . . he was a man in his fifties or so and not real healthy; she was the same age and certainly no threat to anyone . . . the Harpers were tied hand and foot. Trussed like hens going into the oven." Dwight snorted. "It won't be them who roasts in Hell, I'm thinking."

"Bad?" Longarm said.

"Real bad. They pulled Agatha's dress open and burned her, uh, burned her . . ." Dwight's hands fluttered in front of his chest. "Used a hot poker on her or something of the sort. It was ugly. And they didn't put a gag in the mouth of either Aggie nor John. It was clear these people wanted to hear the screaming.

"My guess is that Aggie died before they wanted because they barely got a start on, um, one side. Then they turned to John and did . . . I cannot imagine the sort of man who could do that to another living creature, never mind to another human person."

"That bad," Longarm said.

"Yes. That bad. It's why I was gone so long. Trying to make sense of it. Trying to follow them. They didn't leave a trail, though. I couldn't track them down. And I'm sure they are long since out of my jurisdiction by now."

"Uh-huh. You did the only thing you could do." Longarm said that. He did not believe a word of it.

The killers had not left a trail. Bullshit. Unless they had wings and knew how to fly, they damn sure did leave some sort of trail. It was just that portly Sheriff Dwight was not able to find and follow it.

And out of his jurisdiction? That was an excuse, not a reason. If Custis Long wanted someone badly enough, he would be willing to follow them to the gates of hell itself.

He rather suspected that Tom Dwight would really prefer that he not have to face whoever tortured and killed those people down at Harper's.

Longarm opened his mouth to ask some of the questions that might help him get a handle on the killers. Did they clean out the store's supply of whiskey? Or of tobacco? How much food did they carry away with them? Were weapons or ammunition stolen? What about horses or a wagon?

He changed his mind and said nothing, however. It was clear that Dwight wanted shut of this case, and it was damn sure not Longarm's jurisdiction. No federal crime had been committed so far as he knew, and he had no authority to go scampering off in pursuit of someone else's problems.

His job was to get Jack Handley back to Manitou for trial. Period. Not a single thing more than that.

Longarm muttered some sympathetic shit for Dwight's benefit, then explained the reason he was there.

"That would be your prison wagon parked around back then," the sheriff said.

"Yes, sir, it would."

"All right then. Let's get the paperwork done and you can have him. Naturally, though, if they should fail to hang him in Colorado, we want him back to serve out his sentence here."

"I'm sure the United States government and the state of Colorado would be happy to have him off their hands if that happens." Longarm thought he heard a faint groan coming from the direction of the cells where Handley was listening to this.

"I have some forms here," Dwight said. "Let me mix some fresh ink and we can get started."

Chapter 13

There was something about wearing a badge, Longarm reflected as his team plodded at a slow, steady walk away from Edwardsville.

Tom Dwight was getting up in years. He had a belly now but no stomach, not for the rough business. And lawing was a rough business. There was no getting around that. Lawing showed a man the worst that was inside his fellow man. It was a trade that, in Longarm's opinion, Dwight should have set aside.

The man was certainly old enough to take an honorable retirement. No one would fault him nor think a thing against him for it. Yet he clung to the job. To the badge.

There was something about it—Longarm had noticed it time and time again—that got into even the lowest constable or jail guard, something that kept him in the game.

It was not bossiness, Longarm thought. At least not so very much so. A little maybe. But really, it was a helluva lot more than that.

A gut-deep sense that folks ought to be straight with one another? That had a whole lot to do with it, he believed. A man oughtn't kill his neighbor or take his neighbor's wife. Shouldn't steal or lie or act indecent.

Longarm chuckled right out loud when he realized where his thoughts were taking him. What it came down to him thinking was that, lawman or no, a man should follow those Ten Commandments that Longarm had been hearing about—but seldom seeing—pretty much his whole life long.

Preachers and lawmen, both believers in their own very different ways? Now that he'd thought of it, he kind of wondered. Was that where it came from, that impulse to keep folks safe from the sins of other folks? Should he start thinking about preachers as being his brothers with a different sort of badge?

Uh . . . no. That would be taking this notion a little too far.

Still, there was something in what he was thinking here. Something that made a man want to hold on to his badge and to his ability to make things better.

Damned small ability, Longarm reflected with a sigh. Damned small indeed.

"What are you laughing about?" the friendly murderer and rapist asked from the cage behind Longarm. There was a solid wall of boards between the wagon driver and the prisoners in the cage. That was to keep the prisoners from being able to reach forward and grab the driver, strangle him maybe, and take his keys. It was a serious enough threat. Longarm had known it to be done before on wagons without the wall.

And while Jack Handley was friendly and laughing and pleasant, he was also headed for a hanging. Who was to say he wouldn't murder in order to avoid that unpleasantness, Ten Commandments notwithstanding? So as it was, Handley could sit within a foot or so of Longarm but he could neither see nor reach him.

"What's that?" Longarm asked over his shoulder.

"I asked what you were laughing about."

"Oh, just . . . thinking."

"Good thoughts then," Handley said. "That's nice. I'm sorry I interrupted."

"It wasn't nothing deep. I don't mind."

"May I ask you something, Deputy?"

"You can always ask. What I answer depends on what the question is."

"I'm going to ask you to let me out."

"Damn if you ain't a bold one, Jack Handley. Damn me if you ain't."

He heard laughter from behind the wall. "Not that way. Not, you understand, that I would object if you did set me free. No, what I have in mind is can you please let me out so I can take a crap. I've been holding it since yesterday and I'm about to bust."

"Yeah, that bucket. I can't say as I blame you."

"I see there's some brambles and flowers and things growing along that fence line over there. You could watch me close. Hold a shotgun over me or whatever it is you are obligated to do. But I need to go, Deputy. I need real bad to take a dump."

"I can do better than a squat in the bushes, Jack. Can you see that farmhouse over there? On the right. Do you see it?"

"Yes, why?"

"Because that's where we're going, that's why. I have t' pick up another passenger there. A young lady. I expect I can trust you t' mind your manners with her."

"I should certainly hope so," Handley said.

"Good. Because it would piss me off real bad if you was to grab at her or say lewd things to her or shit like that. An' you don't want t' piss me off, Jack."

"Of course I know how to act around a lady. Now about that crap . . . ?"

"When we get to the farm, I'll ask can you use their

outhouse. I'm not so foolish as to ask for your parole about this, understand. I'm trusting in Sam Colt to keep you in line instead o' Jack Handley or the Ten Commandments."

"Ten Command . . . where did that come from?" Handley asked, clearly puzzled by the comment.

"Oh, uh . . . never mind about that. Just take care that you don't try anything stupid an' you can take your shit an' maybe even walk around for a few minutes before we roll on."

"I would appreciate that, Deputy."

Longarm turned the team up the lane. The horses must have seen the farm buildings and recognized that such places were where grain was kept, for they picked up their speed. They were still traveling at a walk, but it was a brisk walk now.

What the hell. Longarm figured he could reward them each with a handful of the mixed grain he carried under the seat. Let them have that and a drink too before they set off back for Denver to drop Emily off and then on south to Manitou for Handley's fair, unbiased trial . . . and subsequent hanging.

"How bad d'you have to go?" Longarm asked over his shoulder.

"I'm starting to taste it on the back of my tongue, I think."

"All right. I'll let you out first thing when we get there. But mind yourself. Don't give me no trouble or you'll be inside that cage using a bucket the whole rest o' the way back."

"You have my word on it."

Longarm had "had the word" of a fair good many prisoners in the past. Most of them he wouldn't trust anymore than he would take a pledge from Beelzebub himself. There were exceptions, but those were rare, and he was not about to put Jack Handley into that category, never mind how friendly and innocent he seemed. The man could simply be trying to cozy his way into Longarm's good graces and give himself an edge for a breakout. Or not.

The one thing that was sure was that Longarm was not going to take any chances with a convicted rapist and accused murderer.

"Just about there, Handley. I'll swing over an' park beside the outhouse. That should make your run a little shorter."

"Thank you. Thank you."

Now there, Longarm reflected, was sincerity.

He guided the team to a halt beside the outhouse, stepped down, and clipped a hitch weight to the bit of his wheeler, then dragged the huge, heavy key out of his pocket and went around back to open the door and relieve Handley of his misery.

"Emily?" Longarm called out while he fiddled with the lock. "Em? Where are you, girl. Sorry to cut off your visit but we got t' get back now. I've dawdled as long as I can already. Emily? Hey! Come out here an' say hello, will you?"

Longarm heard a loud groan of utter relief come from inside the outhouse.

But he heard nothing from the Balcolm farmhouse.

Chapter 14

"Feel better now?" Longarm asked when the round little elf came out into the sunshine, his face even redder than ever from the straining and grunting that had been going on in there.

"Lord, yes," Handley said. He beamed with the satisfaction of a really good shit. Without asking for Longarm's permission, he went over to the pump to wash his hands, then dried them by the simple expedient of wiping them on the sides of his shirt. "Now where is this lady we are supposed to drive back with us?" he asked when he was done.

"I'd like to know that my own self," Longarm said.

Longarm's intention was to lock Handley back in the cage before he went knocking on the Balcolm family's door, but before he could do that the fat man stepped up onto the farmhouse porch. "Uh-oh."

"What's wrong?" Longarm headed toward the porch too, forgetting for the moment the need to lock Handley away.

"I think . . ." Handley raised his head and sniffed. "Oh, dear."

As Longarm came near he could smell it too, and the scent sent a chill through him.

It was the rank, nasty odor of death. The smell of feces and cold piss and decomposing flesh.

"Oh, shit," he mumbled, his dark and deadly Colt in hand without him consciously willing it to be there. "Stand clear, Jack."

Handley nodded. But moved in close behind Longarm as the tall deputy stepped to the door. Longarm could not tell if Handley was seeking protection there or if the tubby little man wanted to be able to give whatever help he could. Of the two, Longarm rather suspected the latter.

The front door of the house was slightly ajar, and the stink of death was behind it.

Now that they were close, Longarm could hear the drone of bluebottle flies and the skitter of tiny claws on polished wood.

Longarm swung the door open and peered inside without yet stepping into the house.

What he found sickened him. His gut wrenched and twisted, and he felt his gorge rise.

"God," Jack Handley whispered.

Handley brushed past Longarm and went into the house, dropping down to kneel beside the nearer of the two sturdy kitchen chairs where the bodies were tied. The little man very quickly muttered something under his breath, then hurried into the parlor to grab a knitted afghan from the settee and bring it back into the kitchen. He draped the cover over the naked body of a woman.

The dead man tied in the chair beside the woman's was naked from the waist up, and he had suffered the same sort of malicious torture as the gray-haired woman, if perhaps not quite so severely.

Both people, however—Longarm had to assume

they were Mr. and Mrs. Balcolm—had been murdered with slow and deliberate care, their deaths drawn out as painfully as any Apache could have done. Both were covered with puncture wounds and shallow cuts. Their bodies were dark with dried blood, and mice or birds or something had been feeding on the corpses. A fresh hatch of flies swarmed over the bodies, crawling in and out of their mouths and noses.

"The raiders who hit Harper's store," Longarm said. "It has to be the same sons of bitches as did that. And this time they could take their time about it. There's no danger of customers coming here to interrupt them. Just maybe a neighbor dropping by, and they must've figured they could handle that if anybody came."

"What about . . . what about your lady friend?" Handley asked gently. "I see no sign of her."

Longarm grunted, then with Jack Handley trailing, went through the house. He found Emily's bag, but there was no other sign of her. Certainly he did not find her body. She had to have been present when her parents were tortured and killed.

And the killers must have carried her along with them when they left.

Someone to torment and murder at their leisure later on? The thought was maddening.

"Those bastards are . . ." Longarm clamped his mouth closed. He'd turned to comment to Handley, but the fat man was no longer beside him. Longarm had been so preoccupied with his concern for Emily and the thoughts of what might have happened to her—might at that very moment still be happening to her—that he had forgotten about Handley.

Now his prisoner was gone. Vanished without a sound. Damn, but that squat little son of a bitch moved lightly for such a fat man.

Longarm whirled, again palming his revolver. He

glanced quickly through the house, then ran out onto the porch.

Jack Handley was outside in the yard beside the house. He had found a shovel somewhere and was busily starting to dig.

Longarm shoved the Colt back into his holster. "Jack, what the hell are you doin'?"

Handley stopped his efforts long enough to look up and say, "You want to bury those poor souls before we start after the men who did this, don't you? Well, don't just stand there, man. There's another spade in the shed there."

Chapter 15

Longarm took a deep breath and shook himself in an effort to chase some of the aches. He stepped over to the pump and sluiced cold, sweet water over his face and forearms, then cupped his palm and drank until his belly hurt. Digging graves was not a pleasant chore. But it was something that had to be done.

When he straightened and turned around, Jack Handley was standing there. For a moment Longarm had forgotten about his prisoner. Again. There was something about Handley that just did not seem to fit the role of a prisoner, though, something that made the man easy to overlook despite his bulk. "Yes, Jack, what is it?"

"I just wanted to let you know. There are some old saddles in the barn, and one good saddle horse. I took the liberty of saddling the good horse for you and a little cob for myself."

"And why would we be leaving the wagon and switching to the saddle," Longarm asked.

"Whoever did this kidnapped your friend. Someone has to go after them and there isn't anyone to do it except you and me."

"But you are . . ."

"Yes, of course I am, but I can be just as much your prisoner on the trail of those murderers as I can sitting in that prison wagon. Besides, this is your lucky day. Well, so to speak. If I do say so myself, Deputy, I am probably the best tracker you have ever encountered."

"You?" Under other circumstances Longarm would have laughed out loud, but he did not think that would be appropriate standing over the graves of Emily Balcolm's parents.

"I don't wish to be immodest but . . . yes. I am."

Longarm glanced toward the sun, which by now was very low on the horizon. "There isn't much tracking light left."

"All the more reason to be on our way. Now give me a hand, will you? We need to take your wagon team out of harness and pitch some hay down for them. And if you don't mind doing that yourself, I do not get along well with climbing and high places. I would rather not go up into that loft for the hay."

"And you'll give me your parole, I suppose."

"Yes, I will, as a matter of fact. Not that I expect you to put much faith in that, so keep an eye on me. But do it after you come down out of that hayloft. We don't have any time to waste here."

"Those men have at least a two-day head start on us."

"That is all right. Wherever they have gone, I can track them."

Longarm took a deep breath. Then sighed. "Damn you, Handley, you do confuse a man."

The fat man grinned but said nothing.

"All right, damn it. You strip the harness off the wagon team while I toss some hay down into the pen. But mind you, don't do anything out of line. I like you, Jack, but I won't let you escape."

"I would expect no less from you, Deputy. Now get on up there. And be quick about it, will you?"

Longarm was half annoyed and half amused. Handley was his prisoner, dammit. Now the man was giving orders. What a very strange little fellow he was.

"When you're done with those horses, Jack, go inside and see if you can find any food we can carry along and something to carry it in. I'll pack some grain for the horses. We can use one of the horses to carry our stuff. We'd best be prepared, I think, because it may be a while before we see the inside of a store again."

"Good idea. Go on now. I will still be here when you get down."

The horse Longarm was riding was a leggy, hammer-headed idiot creature that was probably much more accustomed to being in harness than under saddle. It had a road gait that would rattle a man's teeth and curdle his innards. It pulled at the bit and invariably tried to bite Longarm's kneecap off every time he tried to mount. It was willful and stubborn and ugly. And at that it was far better than the short, stout little cob that Handley had chosen.

"Damn all farmers anyhow," Longarm mumbled as he followed close behind Handley.

Despite his discomfort and despite the seriousness of the mission they were on, Longarm damn near had to laugh, though, at the sight of the fat little man perched atop a fat little horse, the whole appearance made complete by the three-legged milk stool that Jack Handley carried on his pommel tucked in tight against Jack's more than ample belly.

The stool had a length of rope tied to one end, the other end of the rope secured on the horn of his saddle.

"What the *hell* is that rig for?" Longarm asked the first time he saw it back at the Balcolm farm.

"You'll see," Handley said with a smile.

And so he did.

When they mounted to leave, the two saddle horses plus one of the animals from the wagon team loaded with blankets and their supplies, Longarm did indeed see what the stool was for.

As short as his horse was, Jack Handley's legs were even shorter. Undaunted, he set the stool down and used it to climb into his saddle, then tugged on the rope to pull the stool into his lap.

"D'you have any idea what you look like, doin' that?" Longarm asked.

"Do you have any idea how little I care about appearances?" Handley countered.

"No much, I reckon. You say you're a tracker?"

"There is none better."

"Then you take the lead." Longarm did not mention that he was a better than fair hand himself when it came to tracking. If Handley wandered off the trail left by the murderers, Longarm was sure to spot the error. In the meantime, though, he was content to let Handley take the lead, especially since that kept him in front where Longarm could keep an eye on him. Longarm had no idea how far he could trust this prisoner of his. But he was very likely to find out over the next few days.

"There are five horses," Handley said shortly.

"Five? I only count four."

"Five," Handley said with certainty. "There were four when they arrived. They took the fifth animal from the girl's farm."

"Four killers then," Longarm said.

"One or two of those horses could be pack animals, you know."

"You're right. At least two killers then, maybe as many as four. And so far, everyone I know of who's seen the sons of bitches is dead an' can't tell no tales."

"Given a little time, I think we can correct that,"

Handley said. "They don't seem to be in any great hurry to get away. But then I happen to know, and they might know as well, that Sheriff Dwight's jurisdiction ends just a few miles north of here, and there isn't much in the way of civilization for a good distance after that. They may well think once they cross the county line they are in the clear."

"Not damn likely," Longarm said, his voice and expression both grim.

"No, I think not," Handley said. "We needn't be in a rush either. They have at least two days on us. Our best hope is that they stop to . . . I am sorry to say this, Deputy; I know the lady is a friend of yours . . . but we really have to hope they stop to, um, take advantage of their captive."

"Bastards," Longarm mumbled.

After riding in silence for several miles, Handley turned in his saddle and asked, "Will you get in trouble for following them? After all, you are limited to certain jurisdictions too, aren't you?"

Longarm grunted. "I'll follow 'em to Hell itself if I have to. Besides, a man can receive his mail at Harper's store. That means Harper represented the United States government here. The way I see it, killing him put them square in my gun sights."

"It will be dark soon," Handley said a few minutes later. "We can stop for the night in that copse of trees over there."

"I hate t' stop when we've barely got started, but I reckon you're right. It's soon too dark to read sign. One thing you should know, Jack. I got to get some sleep. We could be at this for a good while, an' I don't want t' wear down, so I need my sleep. That means, for my own peace o' mind, I'm gonna have to put the handcuffs back on you overnight."

"I take no offense," Handley said.

"Good, 'cause there's none intended."

"Follow me then. I think I see a good spot to set up for the night."

Chapter 16

Longarm woke before dawn, sat up in the blankets he had scavenged from the Balcolm farm, and with a huge, shuddering yawn finally stood and stretched.

A dull red glow guided him to the coals of the previous evening's fire, where he hunkered down and used the end of a stick to stir up a little fire, then a bigger one as he fed small pieces of dry wood onto the coals.

The flare of light from the flames found the shine of Jack Handley's eyes at the base of the tree where he was stretched out on the ground, his hands cuffed so that his arms were around the bole of the tree.

"Mornin', Jack. I didn't know you were awake."

"I sleep light."

"Can you hang on there for a minute?"

"I'm not going anywhere," Handley said lightly, adding a chuckle to the comment.

"No, I expect you ain't." Longarm uncapped the water bag and added some to last night's coffee grounds, then set the pot over the fire. "Give this time to hit a boil and we'll have us some coffee. I hate to admit it after all these years, but I don't make good coffee."

"I can attest to that."

"You really believe that or you just trying t' be polite?"

"No, I genuinely agree that you make lousy coffee, Deputy."

"Well, thank you for the honesty anyhow." Longarm paused. "I think." He went over to Handley's tree and knelt to unlock one side of the handcuffs. Handley sat up and rubbed the freed wrist, then held the other out so Longarm could unlock that bracelet too and slip the cuffs into his pocket.

"Feel better?"

"Much, thank you."

Longarm stood, blinked, and seemed to be in deep thought for a moment.

"Is something wrong, Deputy?"

"I just thought . . . last night when you laid down to sleep . . . wasn't that coat you're wearing wadded up for you to use as a pillow?"

Handley looked down at the green plaid wool coat he was wearing, looked at it as if seeing it for the first time, then looked up again. "What an odd thing for you to say," he said.

Longarm hesitated. Then shrugged. The man was right, of course. His hands had been chained around the damned tree. Of course he had to have been wearing the coat when he went to sleep. "Go ahead an' take a leak if you like. Just don't go so far that I think you're trying to get away."

The round little man with the features like those of a Christmas elf began to laugh as he walked off away from the fire to tend to his bodily needs. Longarm settled the coffeepot more securely over the fire, then ambled away in the other direction to take care of his own business.

Breakfast was cold corn cakes that they'd found in the Balcolm kitchen along with weak but terribly bitter coffee. Handley bent his head and prayed before he ate his. Longarm got the impression that it was the man's normal practice and not something he was putting on to make Longarm think he was a pious sort.

"Ready to ride?" Longarm asked when they were done. A thin band of light was visible on the horizon to the east. It would be daybreak soon.

Handley groaned. But he stood and began very efficiently gathering everything, ready to set out again.

"Wait." Handley motioned with his hand for Longarm to stop behind him. "Don't ride over these tracks. Give me a minute to look them over first."

"Can do," Longarm said, settling back in his saddle and pulling out a cheroot. He struck a match and applied it to the cigar, then shook the fire out and tossed the matchstick away once his cheroot was lighted and drawing nicely.

"There are three of them," Handley said. "This is where they spent the night two nights ago. You can see there where they covered up their fire. It wasn't much of a fire to begin with, so they must be afraid someone is following.

"That is . . . I'm sorry, deputy, but over there is where they put the girl. She was tied to that tree. Just her hands, though. She was lying full length on the ground. You can imagine what they did to her. It looks like they took turns. Two of them did anyway. I'm not sure about the third.

"Either they stopped fairly early or they stayed here late the next morning because they put the horses on a picket line overnight . . . you can see the droppings there . . . but there was time for the animals to graze too. Which probably means they didn't think to bring grain along. At least I don't see any dropped kernels, and there surely would be a few even if they fed from nose bags."

"You're sure there are the three plus Emily?"

"Yes. I'm sure," Handley said.

Longarm was sure of it too. He was a more than fair hand at tracking himself. But he had not seen fit to tell Jack Handley that. It was a small precaution, one of those just-in-case things. There was no real need for the prisoner to know that Longarm was fully capable of tracking him if he chose to make a break for it. And Handley really was quite good. The tubby little fellow had brought them along behind the murderers swiftly and surely.

Longarm looked at this campsite now and could scarcely imagine the hell gentle Emily Balcolm had gone through here.

And this on top of having seen her parents murdered, possibly in front of her eyes. The more Longarm thought about it, the angrier he became.

"Let's go, Jack."

"I have to take a piss."

"All right, dammit, but hurry. Hurry."

Chapter 17

"What the devil is this doing here?"

Longarm stared down at a patch of tall weeds and sumac.

"Dumped," Handley said. "I noticed a half mile back that one of their horses started limping. Turned its ankle or got a stone bruise or something. Now this."

They were both looking at a stock saddle. Cheap to begin with, the saddle had seen hard use. It was thorn-scratched and rope-burned, water-stained and sunbaked. It was a working saddle. And while a saddle of this age and condition would not be worth much, it would certainly be worth something. It most definitely was not the sort of thing a man would choose to discard in the bushes. Not without reason.

"It looks to me," Handley said, "like one of them dropped his saddle here, then turned his horse loose. It followed along behind the others, but you can see that it wasn't being led. I'd say it was wandering free. And a lot slower than the other animals. The fellow who'd been riding it moved something . . . my guess would be it was the girl . . . onto the back of a different horse; then he got onto the one she had been riding."

Longarm nodded. That was the way he read it too, although either Jack Handley was one hell of a lot better at reading sign than Longarm, or the fat man was making some guesses. Probably guessing at least a little, Longarm concluded, but then there was nothing wrong with that. An awful lot of successful tracking involved successful guesswork and a basic knowledge of human nature.

"So the four people and their pack goods are all piled onto just the four horses," Longarm said. "I wonder why they dumped this saddle instead o' the pack frame. They could've distributed their supplies around an' switched this saddle onto the packhorse. I wonder why they didn't."

"Sometimes people do things without good reason," Handley said. He shook his head. "Sometimes they do things that are just plain stupid. You can't always figure that sort of thing out."

"Whatever their reason . . . if they even had one . . . it looks to be good news for us. They are traveling heavier now. That means they're apt t' go slower, stop earlier." Longarm scowled. "Have more time to share Emily around amongst 'em."

"Yes. I'm sorry, Deputy."

"Forget the saddle, Jack. Let's go."

Handley nodded and bumped his horse in the ribs to send it into a walk again.

"There!"

"What?"

"Stay still," Longarm ordered, dragging his Winchester from the scabbard slung under his knee. "I want you t' wait here. Don't take a step toward me unless I call you, and for damn sure don't try and move away from me or I'll have t' shoot you. D'you understand what I'm telling you, Jack?"

"Yes, of course, but what is wrong?"

"Maybe nothing, but maybe something is. I'm pretty sure I saw something move over there in that thicket of quakies. Could've been a deer flicking its ear. Could've been some son of a bitch with a rifle. You stay here while I find out."

"I won't take a step in any direction," Handley swore solemnly.

"You better not." Longarm swung his horse around and put it into a lope. He made a wide circle around the quakies until he could approach through cover, then slowed down and moved in as silently as he could.

He took a good half hour to make his approach. Then he cussed and called out, "You can come down here now, Jack. There's no danger."

Handley had sat on his short-legged little animal without moving for the entire time.

At least the man was obeying orders, Longarm thought . . . when he believed he was being watched anyway. The truth, however, was that Longarm had not been able to pay attention to Jack Handley while he was stalking what might have been an ambusher.

If Handley had chosen to make a break for it at that moment, there would have been hell to pay. And he very likely would have gotten clean away, at least for the time being. There was no way Longarm would abandon Emily Balcolm just so he could transport a prisoner to the jail in Manitou. Handley would have had to wait.

"What is it?" the chubby fellow asked, stroking his beard to smooth down the whiskers.

Longarm did not bother to answer, merely inclined his head toward the quakies. After a moment Handley grunted and said, "Oh. Darn."

They had caught up with the lamed horse the murderers abandoned some miles back. It was peacefully grazing.

"What should we do with it?" Handley asked.

"Nothing. If it's something minor that's gone wrong, it will heal over time. If it's something more serious, well, I ain't gonna be responsible for putting down some other man's horse. It don't bother me a whole helluva lot to shoot men, but I purely dislike having to kill a horse, even out of kindness."

Handley looked at him for a moment, then grunted again. "This light won't last very much longer," he said. "We should make what progress we can before dark."

Longarm nodded and reined his mount back toward the trail the kidnappers had taken.

Chapter 18

It was nearly dark when they topped a low ridge line overlooking a broad, shallow valley.

"Likely there's farms down there or some cow outfits," Longarm said, "but it's too dark to see very far, an' anyway I don't want to risk losing the trail. We'll sleep out tonight instead o' looking for a roof to get under."

"All right. Where?"

Longarm inclined his head back the way they had just come. "South side of this ridge," he said. "I seen a little seep back there where we oughta be able to collect enough water for some coffee an' to fill the canteen."

"Won't that be going in the wrong direction?" Handley asked.

"Couple hundred yards is all and won't nobody be able to see our fire," Longarm responded.

"Do you think we are that close to them?"

"No. But it never hurts to be careful. I expect we'll catch up with them tomorrow or the day after, depending on how early they stop. They'll be wanting to get at Emily. You can be sure of that. That's why they brought her along, don't forget. And they'll each be wanting their share of her."

"You take this calmly enough, Deputy, knowing what those men will be doing to your friend."

"Calm? No. Not a bit of it. But blustering and roaring and making a show of what I'm feeling won't do anything for her. Catching up with those bastards will."

"And then?"

"That will be up to them. Over here." He turned his horse parallel to the slope and continued a rod or two to a depression in the earth where a trickle of sweet water emerged from the hillside. "We'll stop here." Longarm stepped down from his horse. Handley carefully eased down to the ground beside him.

They tended to the animals first; then Longarm found wood and built a fire while Handley unloaded their bedrolls and gear and began putting together a meal, starting with that pot of coffee.

After they ate, Longarm hunkered beside the fire with one of his very few remaining cheroots while Jack Handley sat cross-legged in the grass nearby. "Do you mind if I ask you something, Deputy?"

"Go ahead."

"What will you do with those men when you catch up with them?"

"Arrest them and take them in for trial, of course. Why?"

"I thought maybe that's what you would say, but I wanted to hear it from you. I just want you to know that tomorrow or the whenever we find them, you can count on me to help with whatever needs to be done. I don't countenance rape."

"Coming from you, Jack, that's a funny thing t' hear, you bein' a convicted rapist your own self."

"I told you what happened at that farm. If you want to call it rape, feel free."

"And the fellow in Manitou? You said you shot him."

"So I did, Deputy, so I did."

"You never said why you shot him."

"No, I suppose I didn't."

"Well?"

"Well, what?"

"I . . . never mind."

Handley nodded, then yawned and stretched. "If you don't mind, Deputy, I think I'll bed down now. I'm not used to riding so far. Not astride anyway."

"I'll have to cuff you again, Jack, like I done last night."

"That's fine. Let me fix my bed. At the base of that tree perhaps? Will that be all right?"

"Fine by me." Longarm pulled the manacles from his pocket and followed the prisoner to his preferred tree. Handley lay down on his belly with one hand extended on either side of a small pine and Longarm snapped the steel bracelets in place.

"Good night, Deputy."

"G'night, Jack."

Longarm fell asleep almost immediately. He woke sometime short of dawn, his eyes snapping open and hand reaching for the always present Colt revolver, all traces of sleep driven from him. Something was moving in the grass nearby.

Something . . . "Well, shit." He sat up and shoved the .44-.40 back into his holster.

"Oh. Sorry. I didn't mean to wake you."

"Jack, you . . . Good Lord, man, what are you doing over there!"

"I had to take a piss. Real bad. Sorry."

"But you . . . dammit, Jack, I handcuffed you around that tree. You can't be loose now."

"Really? Then I suppose I am still there." Handley leaned down to drop a few pieces of wood onto the fire, then went back to his bedroll. He lay down and, yawning, slipped the handcuffs back onto his own wrists. "See? Still there."

"How the hell did you do that?"

Handley grinned. Slid his right hand out of the handcuff bracelet, scratched the side of his nose, and promptly handcuffed himself again.

"For God's sake, man," Longarm yelped.

Jack Handley's grin grew wider. "It's sort of a parlor trick."

"Some parlor."

"I've always been something of a prestidigitator, and . . ."

"A what?"

"A magician. Sort of. I'm just an amateur at it really. But between that and tending to be rather good with locks, if I do say so, well, you can see how one thing might lead to another."

"Could you have gotten out of that cell back in Edwardsville?"

"I am sure I could have, although I didn't try."

"And you've been able to slip those cuffs all along?"

"Of course."

"But you didn't make a run for Canada or anything like that."

"No, why should I?"

"You were convicted of a serious crime, Jack. You could spend the rest of your life behind bars. Worse, that life might be mighty short if they convict you for murder when we get to Manitou."

"They won't."

"Why would you say that? You yourself told me that you killed the man."

"But I never said I murdered him. Can we go back to sleep now? We don't need to get up yet, and I don't know about you but I for one am awfully tired after that long ride."

"Fine, but . . ."

"I have faith, Deputy." Handley rolled over, scratched

his belly with a hand that was supposed to be shackled securely around that tree, then returned his hand to confinement again. He looked at Longarm and smiled. "You will think of something to help. I know you will."

"Dammit, Jack."

Handley did not answer, and a minute or so later his breathing deepened and soon he began to snore.

It took Longarm considerably longer to drop back to sleep.

Chapter 19

"Over this way," Handley said, turning in the saddle and leaning on the stool that he continued to use as his stepladder to the stirrup. "The trail is over here."

"In a minute then," Longarm said. "I smell something over this way."

Handley shook his head. "You 'smell' something? Does that mean you see some sort of sign or clue that I missed?"

"No, it means I actually smell something, Jack. I hope t' hell I'm wrong, but it smells like something I've come across way too damn often before. Now give me just a minute, will you?"

"Oh, shit," Longarm grumbled a minute later when he broke through a clump of sumac to find a man's body lying curled in a fetal position, his clothes covered with blood and old leaf litter. He had been gut-shot and must have been in agony before he died.

A trail of scuff marks showed that he had crawled here from some little distance away, but there was no blood trail to show where that had been. Apparently, he had not hemorrhaged and bled out until sometime after he was shot.

"Well, shit," Handley agreed.

Both men dismounted, and Longarm leaned down close to the dead man to look him over.

"One of the killers?" Handley asked. "Did they have a falling-out among themselves?"

"It could be, I suppose."

"Why would he be barefoot? There is no sign that anyone camped here overnight, and we know that the killers did not."

"If you look around, you'll probably find a pair of discarded boots. Prob'ly one of the murderers liked this fella's boots better'n their own."

"And that is why they killed him?"

Longarm only shrugged. "I tell you, though, Jack, I don't want t' take time to bury him, all the more so because he might could be from around here. He might have folks nearby who need to mourn him an' do the burying."

"What makes you think he lives . . . lived, I mean . . . close around here?"

Longarm gestured down at the dead man lying pale and cold at their feet. "Clean clothes," he said. "Underneath the blood and what's on him from wallowing around on the ground, those clothes are clean. I'd think our fellas would be pretty grimy by now, riding out away from towns and baths and what-not. This man is fresh-shaved and looks like he got a haircut fairly recently too."

"So you think he is another victim?"

"Uh-huh."

"Are we going to take time to bury him?"

Longarm hesitated. "No. If those sons of bitches are still intent on killing people, we got to catch up with them quick as possible lest they do any more of this."

Handley nodded. He bent down and plucked a bandanna kerchief out of the dead man's back pocket, then tied the flaming red square of cloth on a limb as high as he could reach.

"Good idea," Longarm said, then sighed. "I wish there was something around here we could cover him up with, something to keep the crows and the foxes off him."

"I could get my blanket to lay over him," Handley suggested. "I can get along without it."

"That's nice of you, Jack, but they'd only slip underneath a blanket or tug it off. We'll just let the poor son of a bitch lay where he is an' hope it won't be long before we get back to him."

Longarm mounted and waited patiently while Jack Handley set his stool in place so he too could crawl into the saddle. Handley used the cord tied on his saddle horn to lift the stool, carefully coiled the cord, and nestled the stool in his lap. "All right, I'm ready now."

A few minutes later, when they returned to more open ground, Handley turned and said, "The dead man was not any part of the gang. You can see here where they stopped him. He was on horseback. They shot him . . . I would say right there. You can see where he fell down and rolled on the ground. And he had a horse. They took the horse and whatever else they wanted. Anyway, they have replaced that horse that went lame."

"Could be why they shot the fella t' begin with," Longarm said. "I wouldn't be surprised."

"I wish I could say that I am shocked. Or even a little bit surprised. I can't. Not when it comes to this bunch. These are ugly people, Deputy. It saddens me to say that about anyone, but I fear that it is true." He shook his head. "Ugly, ugly people."

"Then you an' me had best move along an' catch up with them, Jack."

"These men are killers, Deputy. Cold-blooded killers. And you are only one man."

"Yeah, but ain't it written down somewhere that one righteous man is worth ten sons of bitches like them?"

Handley chuckled. "I never heard it put in exactly those words before but, yes, I do seem to recall something like that, Custis."

Longarm was not sure—and it did not mean anything anyway—but he believed that was the first time Jack Handley ever called him by name. "C'mon, Jack. An' this time you can follow me. We're fixing to make some time." He put the spurs to his horse and heard a yelp behind him as his prisoner rushed to catch up.

Chapter 20

Longarm stopped, giving his horse a breather. Jack Handley rode up beside him before he too reined to a halt. Longarm inclined his head eastward along the valley where they found themselves and said, "That's where they'll be headed."

"You think so?"

"Aye. There's a town or village over there. You can see the smoke from the fires where folks are cooking supper. The gang will be headed there, I guarantee it. They'll be wanting drinks and hot food cooked on a stove and soft beds t' sleep in. Maybe baths too and fresh women for themselves if they got money enough for whoring."

"What about your friend?"

Longarm did not answer, and after a moment Handley repeated the question, drawing an anguished look from the tall deputy.

"I've seen cases where captives actually turned to the side of their captors an' tried to help them, stayed with them when they could've got away. I've seen that time an' again. Or they could tie her up an' leave her outside town while they go in an' have themselves a blowout.

Or . . . or could be things got worse for her. We'll see. We'll just have t' go down there an' find them. Do we catch up with them, Jack, I expect they'll tell me what I need to know. I really think they will." Longarm's voice and his expression were grim.

"We're running out of daylight, Custis. Should we continue to follow the trail or cut straight down to the town?" Handley asked.

"Dammit, Jack, I don't mind it when some pretty little gal calls me Custis, but I ain't much used to growed men doing it. Call me Longarm like everyone else does, would you?"

Handley grinned. "Now that you have issued the invitation, I will be proud to call you by that name . . . Longarm."

"That's better. An' in answer to your question, let's put the spurs to these nags an' get on down there while we still got a little daylight remaining." Longarm set the example by gigging his mount into a lope headed straight toward the eastern end of the broad valley. Jack Handley had to scurry to catch up with him.

Despite their efforts, it was already dark by the time they rode onto the bare, rutted strip of dark earth that served the burg as a main street. Most stores were dark and empty, with lights showing only from living quarters perched overhead on second stories, or from windows at the back of the buildings suggesting that the owners lived there. The exceptions were two saloons, one at each end of town, and light coming from the windows of a barbershop beside the nearer of the saloons.

"There," Longarm said, reining his horse toward the barbershop. He could see there were several customers inside, and one man, his face covered with a towel, lying back in the barber chair.

"Do you think . . . ?"

"Damn if I know, Jack, but I want you t' stay back here outa the way while I go in."

"All right."

Longarm dismounted, and Handley slid down to the ground as well. They tied their horses to a rail in front of the shop, and Handley stayed back while Longarm stepped inside the barbershop.

The place smelled of soap and scented lotions. The barber was a thin, graying man who looked up and said, "You're next in line if you like, mister. These other gents are just waiting for the card game to start as soon as I get done with Harry here."

"You fellas all live here, do you?" Longarm asked.

"Yes, indeed we do. Finest prospect in the territory, I'm here to tell you. Are you looking for a place to raise some beef perhaps?" the barber asked.

"No, but I'd like t' know if you've had any strangers come through earlier today."

The barber gave a nervous glance past Longarm toward the front door and swallowed hard. "I, uh, I don't want any trouble."

"No trouble," Longarm said. "I'm a deputy United States marshal."

"Can you prove that?"

Longarm nodded. He reached inside his coat and produced his wallet, which he flipped open to display his badge.

"What about . . . mister, Marshal I mean . . . guns make me awfully nervous. Is he a deputy too?" The man nodded toward the front of his shop.

Longarm turned his head. Jack Handley was standing in the doorway. He had retrieved Longarm's Winchester from the saddle scabbard and was standing there holding it canted across his broad belly. The carbine looked dark and very deadly in Handley's hands.

"Jesus!" Longarm blurted, appalled at the idea of his prisoner, a convicted rapist and accused murderer, standing there armed and unfettered. "Put that thing away, Jack. Put it back where you got it."

"All right." Handley grounded the carbine, but did not take it back to its proper place on the horse.

Longarm returned his attention to the barber. "You was about t' tell me if you've had any customers today that aren't from around here."

"Yes. There were three."

"They all come in at the same time, did they?" Longarm was quite frankly hoping that at least one would have to stay back and stand guard over Emily wherever they went and whatever they did.

The barber nodded. "Yes. They've been traveling, that much was clear. They paid cash money for haircuts, shaves, and baths, all three of them. They brought clean clothes with them. The shirts had creases in them from lying on a shelf and they were the sort of shirts that Sam Whittby sells. Same britches too."

"Denims?"

"That's right."

"New ones, you say."

"Yes. They put on the new when they were done washing and left their old things for me to throw away. They were pretty thoroughly tattered and to tell you the truth, they did not smell any too good either."

Longarm permitted himself a tight smile. The murderers did not know it, but they were being almighty helpful. New jeans, dark blue and stiff as boards, would stand out in any crowd.

"I don't suppose you remember what colors those shirts were, do you?"

"You are chasing those men, aren't you? What did they do, Marshal?"

Longarm ignored the question. "The shirts?"

"They are all the same. Red and a black houndstooth pattern. Nice shirts, and the color holds up after a good bit of washing. I know. I have one of those shirts myself." He smiled. "Sam's order got mixed up somehow and all the shirts in that shipment were the same color and pattern. Half the men around here are wearing them."

But not new, iron-stiff britches, Longarm thought.

"Where would they be staying?"

"They didn't tell me, Marshal, but if they hired rooms there wouldn't be much choice. We don't have a proper hotel, but the Tomkin twins take in boarders when there are strangers passing through."

"There's rooms to be had behind the saloon next door too," one of the customers put in.

The barber snorted. "Cribs, you mean."

Whatever they were called, Longarm was betting that was where he would find his men.

"Will you be staying over?" the barber asked.

Longarm had already turned on his heel and was heading for the doorway and the saloon next door. He did not pause to respond. The stony set of his expression and the tension that bristled the hairs on the back of his neck suggested that his thoughts at the moment were far from any concern about overnight accommodations.

Chapter 21

The saloon had a low ceiling and poor light that came from lamps affixed on the walls. Several of the lamps were unlighted, though, and all had dirty, carbon-stained globes that cut down on the amount of light they gave off.

There were card tables scattered here and there on the floor and a long bar across the entire width of the back wall. The place smelled of beer and sawdust. To Longarm's mind it was a homey, actually quite pleasant scent.

At least a score of men were crowded into the room, a few sitting at the tables, most helpfully holding up the planks of the bar with their elbows. At the far right end of the bar, standing very slightly apart from everyone else in the room, were a pair of hard cases wearing the red-and-black-checked shirts—four others in the room also wore those same shirts, although theirs looked to have been laundered a time or two since they were new, and most importantly, they had no brand-new, dark-blue jeans that still bore the creases from being piled on Sam Whittby's store shelf.

Both hard cases had blond hair so pale it was almost

white, and ruddy, sun-reddened faces. Both had recent haircuts and were freshly shaved. They were almost certain to be brothers.

Only two, Longarm reflected with relief. That meant one of them—a third brother perhaps?—was probably detailed to watch over Emily while the others had their evening's entertainment.

That entertainment included the companionship of one of the two whores who were working the room.

Two whores. Longarm frowned when he saw that. Surely a town this size could support more than two middle-aged, dirt-cheap floozies. Perhaps the third killer was occupied back in one of the cribs and Emily . . . he did not want to think about what that could mean. He really preferred to believe that she was alive and well and still being held captive.

Whatever had happened to her, though, he damn sure intended to find out. Starting right about . . .

"You men!" Longarm's voice, cold and hard and carrying an unmistakable edge of authority, cut through the soft buzz of conversations within the saloon, immediately capturing the attention of the patrons with one exception. A drunk off to his left continued talking about the price of seed until someone else jabbed the man with an elbow to shut him up.

"You," Longarm repeated, fixing the two suspects with a chilling stare. "I am placing you under arrest, both of you. The charges will be murder, robbery, kidnapping, we'll see whatever else the lawyers can come up with. Keep your hands where I can see them, turn around, an' stand right where you are against that bar. You, lady, move out from between them two. Move slow if you please.

"The rest of you"—he raised his voice to reach the rest of the crowd of evening revelers, although that was not really necessary; the only sounds in the place were the ones he was making—"the rest o' you please stay where you are. I don't wanta mistake an innocent motion for a threat an' put a bullet into you by accident.

"You two. Hands high an' turn around, I said."

"Shee-it!" one of the men said. He reached for his gun. His partner reached for the whore, grabbing her by the throat and jerking her against his body as a shield.

The man drawing his revolver was surprisingly fast. Much faster than Longarm. The fellow's hand flashed and his Colt appeared there as if by magic. Flame and hot lead spit from the muzzle before Longarm's .44-.40 cleared leather.

The man was fast. But his concentration over what must have been countless hours had been spent on speed instead of accuracy. The lance of flame that blasted out of his gun barrel was tilted high. His bullet tore into the ceiling, sending a cascade of splinters down onto the crowd below.

Longarm's big Colt roared an instant later.

But his bullet went nowhere near the low ceiling.

It struck the blond gunman square in the forehead, snapping his head backward. Or what was left of his head. A good portion of that body part was blown outward, splattering the walls with bits of starkly white bone and pink and gray brains.

A fair amount of the gray, greasy brain matter ended up distributed wet and sticky on the whore's painted face and powdered bosom and on one side of the face of the instantly dead gunman.

The quick-draw artist's revolver clattered to the plank flooring and his body fell on top of it, landing with a dull thump.

"No!" the remaining brother shrieked.

Still holding the whore by the throat, he pulled his gun too.

Longarm wanted to arrest these sons of bitches,

dammit. He wanted to talk to them. He wanted them to tell him where he could find Emily. He did *not* want to shoot them.

Still, he had no choice in the matter. He either had to shoot back or stand there and wait to be shot himself. And he had little in the way of a target to aim at with the whore's rather ample body being held close against that of the rampaging murderer.

Again Longarm took a head shot, snapping his second round off before the blond gunman had time to aim.

Again the result was messy. Blood, brain, and bone flew as one entire side of the man's head exploded under the impact of Longarm's bullet.

The whore screamed, and the man who had been holding her collapsed onto the floor behind her. The falling body rolled forward, striking the whore behind her knees and bringing her down to the floor too.

Longarm took a step forward.

Then whirled as he heard the explosion of another gunshot close *behind his back*.

Chapter 22

Longarm had his Colt cocked and ready to blast Jack Handley in the chest when he heard a thump and a clatter on the far side of the room. Handley was still holding Longarm's Winchester, but the barrel was pointed in the direction of the sounds and a thin wisp of smoke rose curling from the muzzle. Longarm dropped into a crouch and spun in the direction of the sounds.

He saw an overturned chair and the body of a youngster with pale blond hair sprawled across a poker table. Blood ran from a wound in the dead man's chest, soaking the cards and chips and green felt covering on the table. Two other men, one of them still holding a set of five cards clutched in his fist, stood with their hands raised.

The dead man, Longarm saw, wore a red-and-black-checked shirt . . . and brand-new jeans.

A nickel-plated revolver lay on the floor where the dead man must have dropped it.

"He had that popgun aimed at your back," Handley said calmly. "I didn't think that was very sporting."

"I thought I told you t' put that damned rifle back in my scabbard."

"Mm, yes, I suppose you did." Handley smiled. And very carefully lowered the hammer to safe-cock.

Longarm took a deep breath, then looked around the room before he flipped the loading gate open on his Colt, ejected the spent cartridges, and thumbed fresh rounds into the cylinder.

"I don't know about you," Jack Handley said, "but I think I could use a drink. Mind loaning me two bits so I can buy a couple shots?"

"Loan, hell. You just saved my bacon. I'm buying."

"I will nae say no," the prisoner said in a more than fair imitation of a Gaelic burr.

Longarm looked at the Winchester, shook his head in mock disgust, and held his hand out. Handley gave him the offending firearm, and Longarm led the way through the stunned crowd to reach the bar.

"Mister . . . mister . . . I, uh . . ." The bartender seemed more than a little shaken by the sudden violence in his place. Apparently, the town was not accustomed to this sort of bloodshed.

"It's all right," Longarm said. "I'm a deputy United States marshal. These men were wanted for murder and robbery and half a damn dozen other charges. They just saved the government the cost of a trial in exchange for the price of a few cartridges."

"Who are . . . I mean, who were they?"

"Damn if I know," Longarm said. "You heard them speak to each other by name?"

The barkeep shook his head. "If they did, I didn't pay any mind."

"One of them is called Herk. Or Hack. Something like that," an onlooker put in.

"Which one?" Longarm asked.

The local man shrugged. "I don't recall. Sorry."

"I guess it don't matter," Longarm said. "They can be buried in potter's field under John Doe markers." He turned to the fellow who tried to help with the name. "Go get your local sheriff or town marshal, please. I'll have a drink waiting for you here when you get back."

"All right, thanks." The fellow hurried away. Longarm turned to Handley and held his shot of whiskey up in salute. "Thank you, Jack. I owe you one."

"I'm not expecting anything," Handley said. Then he too raised his glass and tossed back the fiery liquor.

Chapter 23

Longarm displaced one of the whores from her crib—no one in the place seemed inclined to argue with him about it—so they would have a place to sleep. He knew good and well there was no practical purpose to it, but he handcuffed Handley to the cot anyway to remind the fat man that he was supposed to be a prisoner and not some sort of assistant deputy. In deference to Jack's age and awkward girth, though, Longarm gave him the cot while Longarm himself stretched out on the floor.

When Longarm woke in the morning, Jack was already up, sitting on one end of the cot smoking one of Longarm's cheroots and patiently waiting. The handcuffs were carefully folded together and placed on top of Longarm's coat.

"Dammit, Jack," were the first words Longarm uttered in the new day.

Handley grinned. "Good morning, friend Longarm."

Longarm could only shake his head. The hell with it, he decided. He got up, stretched a few of the overnight kinks out of his back, and found another cheroot in his coat pocket. In fact, he found more of the slim cigars than he remembered being in there to begin with.

"What'd you do, go shopping this morning?" he asked.

Handley shrugged. "You were running low."

"Jack! Dammit, no. Prisoners ain't supposed t' do shit like that. An' no-damn-body can move so light as to get around me when I'm sleeping."

"If you say so."

"Damn it anyway," Longarm complained. Futilely, which he already knew.

"There is only one way I could do that," Handley said.

"And that would be . . . ?"

"You do not consider me to be a threat. That is why you were able to relax and sleep so deeply with me in the room." He laughed. "Of course it helped that I was in chains." Handley stood. "I don't know about you, Longarm, but I am awfully hungry this morning."

"Let's go find us a café where we can get some breakfast. At least we agree on that."

"Excellent. Oh, and by the way, Sheriff Dwight impounded all my cash. I had to borrow some of yours to buy those cigars."

"Shit, I s'pose I'm just lucky you didn't take a little extra an' get yourself a blow job while you were at it."

Handley's eyes went wide. "You were awake then?"

Longarm stopped. Stared at the rotund little man. Then felt like the fool when Handley broke into belly-wobbling laughter at the look in Longarm's eyes.

At that point Longarm was not honestly sure if Handley really had used Longarm's money to pay one of the whores for services. Or if he was just pulling Longarm's leg. And he was damn sure not going to ask. "C'mon, Jack, let's go find us some breakfast."

After they ate—in a hole-in-the-wall café that turned out to be surprisingly good and pleasantly cheap—they retrieved the horses from the shed where they had stashed them overnight.

Longarm's expression was serious as he swung into the saddle and waited for Handley to set his milk stool in place so he could climb into the saddle.

"I'm gonna need your tracking abilities t' help me out today, Jack."

It took Jack a moment to understand what Longarm meant. "We have to back-trail those men, don't we. We have to find your friend."

"That's right."

The little man became somber also. "They might have just dumped her when they were tired of her. She could still be alive."

"They might've done a lot o' things, Jack. What you an' me got to do now is find out what they actually done."

"Then I will take the lead if you don't mind. We know what direction they probably entered the town from. We will make some half circles out that way and see if we can pick up their tracks. We won't stop until we find the lady."

Longarm nodded. "Go ahead, Jack."

"Jesus. Shit. Oh, damn it anyway." There was pain reflected in Longarm's voice. He sat with his hands crossed on top of the saddle horn, visibly shaken by the ugliness Jack Handley had led him to.

Emily Balcolm, that sweet and gentle and laughing soul, was dead.

He had expected that. He had not anticipated the brutality of the way she had died. She lay naked in the dirt, her body bruised and torn. She had been mutilated with knives and violated as well with a piece of broken tree limb.

Jack Handley slid down to the ground and used his own blanket to cover her.

"They were more than likely trying to make the murder look like an Indian depredation," Handley said. "That is why—"

"I wish now I hadn't killed them," Longarm growled.

That took Handley aback. "You wish . . ."

"What I wish is that they was alive. So I could fetch them out here an' one by one do all the things to them that they done to Emily."

"I am sorry, Longarm, so very sorry. She was close to you?"

"Yeah. You could say that." Longarm swung down from his saddle. He took a few deep breaths and to all outward appearances returned to being his normal self afterward. He put this behind him and was prepared to get on with life while he still had it. "Those sons o' bitches wiped out the whole family. There's no one to take her back to, Jack. I expect we should just bury her here. There's . . . there's a nice spot over there in that glade. Real pretty. It's the sort o' place she woulda liked."

"All right. Show me where you want me to dig."

They had no spade with them, so Handley rummaged in the packs for the enameled steel tableware they were carrying. Cups and bowls were useful for more than holding coffee or beans, after all.

Chapter 24

It was the middle of the morning four days later when they rode into Edwardsville, again driving the prison wagon that they had left at the Balcolm farm. Jack Handley was again being held inside the cage, but Longarm had appropriated some upholstered pillows from the farmhouse to make the prisoner more comfortable.

And he had taken the Winchester away from Handley. Again.

"This is not a place that I am happy to see," Handley commented from his easy seat behind Longarm.

"Can't say as I blame you, Jack, but I got business here." He could hear Handley's sigh, but paid no attention to it. The day had not yet come when he was going to start letting his prisoners make decisions about where they would be taken or what would be done with them.

Longarm brought the rig to a halt in the street behind the courthouse and hopped down to the ground, then reached back into the driving box for a pair of hitching weights that he dropped under the heads of the horses. He clipped the leather tethers to the horses' bits and ambled down the stairs to the door leading in to Sheriff Dwight's basement office.

"Damn." The door was locked and there was no sign of Dwight.

Longarm mumbled and grumbled his way up to the county clerk's office, where he found the same fellow behind the counter, this time bent over a stack of forms. He was sorting through them, adding comments to some and placing others in a separate pile. He was not too busy to look up when Longarm came in, however.

"I thought you left us a week or so back, Marshal."

"An' so I did. Had to come back through this way, though. D'you know where the sheriff might've got to this time?"

"At this time of day, I would expect him to be over at the store having his coffee and jawing with the fellows. There's a bunch of them that gathers around the stove there, winter or summer, hot or cold. They get together every morning but Sunday." The clerk smiled. "Tell the same yarns over and over too. Are you going to add to their repertoire?"

"Their what?"

"Their, you know, their stock of things to talk about."

"Oh. I expect that I will then. Unfortunately."

"Bad news?"

"Some bad, some good. Maybe they already know about some of it, though." He was thinking about the slaughter out at the Balcolm farm. Neighbors might already have discovered and reported that. "Thank you for your help."

"Any time, Marshal. I'm almost always here. Sad to say."

"Unlike some people," Longarm said. He touched the brim of his hat in silent salute and went out the front of the courthouse, leaving Jack Handley still inside the bars of the prison wagon.

Longarm strode down the quiet, dusty block and into the mercantile. The place smelled of liniment and horehound candy, of smoked hams and new leather. It was cool inside and comfortable, and there were five aging men sitting in a semicircle close to the stove, which at this time of year was unlighted and covered with grease to keep it from rusting. One of the men was Sheriff Tom Dwight. All five became silent and stared at him when Longarm approached.

"I thought you left a long time ago," Dwight said by way of a greeting.

"Ayuh, so I did. Now I'm back. Has anybody reported to you about the Balcolm family?"

Dwight remained seated, his legs comfortably crossed and a pipe between his teeth streaming smoke. "What about them?"

"They was murdered."

"Shit. No. Murdered, you say?"

"Ayuh. Man, wife, and daughter all three. That was all of them, I believe."

"There's a boy away at school," one of the sheriff's cronies put in. "You'll have to tell him, Tom."

"Or somebody will," Dwight said. "We'll get the preacher to do it. He ought to know how to take care of such things." He turned his attention back to Longarm. "You can tell me about it on our way out there. We'll start an investigation into this right away."

"No need for me to go back there, and you can take your time too, Sheriff. The men who did the murders are dead. They're the same ones who did those killings at . . . what's the name of that crossroads store where you were looking into things when I was here before?"

"Harper's, do you mean?"

"That's the place. Same bunch as killed those folks. But all three are all dead now. I caught up with them three days north of here."

"And they are dead? Three of them?"

"That's right."

121

"You killed them all three?"

"That's right too." Longarm did not think it sensible to explain that the sheriff's convicted rapist had shot one of the trio. That confession would surely have led to some awkward explanations and no little embarrassment.

"I appreciate you telling me this, Deputy, uh, Long, wasn't it?"

"Yes, sir."

"Thank you for letting us know."

"Now I need to put my prisoner back into your jail overnight if you will permit it, Sheriff."

"I thought you said they were all dead."

"The murderers are, but I still have the man you turned over to me."

"Oh, yes. Him. Of course you can leave him with me for as long as you like."

"Overnight should do it, I think, but I thank you for the offer."

"Tell me," the sheriff said, taking Longarm by the elbow and leading him out, "are there any rewards outstanding on those men? That is . . . well, I know you federal boys can't collect reward money yourselves. Some of us county and town lawmen can."

"Sheriff, I don't even know who they were, much less if there was paper on them. All I know is that they looked like brothers and that they was stupid."

"Then what about their horses and saddles and other possessions? Did you bring them along? If you turn them over to me, I can sell them for you." Dwight winked. "You and I could share in the proceeds of a thing like that."

"I never thought about that. I got no idea where their gear was nor what's become of it now."

"Damn," Dwight grumbled. "Then why'd you come back here anyway?"

"I still got a little business in these parts. I won't be in your hair for long."

"All right. But I wish you brought all that back with you."

"Come to think of it," Longarm said as they rounded the courthouse and came in sight of the prison wagon where Jack Handley sat waiting, "come to think of it, what did you do with that fella's gear?" He pointed with his chin to indicate Handley. "Did you auction it off or sell it yourself or what?"

"Actually, I just let his victim keep it. As compensation for being wronged, you might say. It seemed the Christian thing to do seeing as how it was his little girl who was violated by that son of a bitch." Dwight raised his voice when he got to "son of a bitch" so as to make sure Handley could clearly hear the comment.

"Horse, wagon, clothes, whatever else was in the outfit? The farmer kept all of that?"

"So he did. Like I told you, it seemed only right, although normally I would have confiscated those things myself." Dwight managed to sound proud of himself for allowing someone else to steal something he normally would have stolen himself.

Longarm stepped to the back of his rig and brought out his key. "With your permission, Sheriff, I'll put Handley back in your cell then."

"You will reimburse the county for his keep, won't you? Fifty cents a day is what we feed. And, uh, another fifty cents for use of the cell. You understand."

Longarm did indeed understand. Sheriff Dwight was disappointed about losing out on those killers' horses and guns and whatnot, but he intended to salve the hurt by getting a little something from the federal government.

"I'll give you a voucher for the cost of housing my

prisoner," Longarm said. He also made a mental note to himself to have Henry make sure that voucher was checked when it came through for approval. Just to make sure there were no claims on it other than the one dollar Longarm agreed to pay.

Not that he was pointing any fingers. But it never hurts to be careful. Longarm took Handley by the elbow to steady him as the fat man scrambled down to the ground and headed for the familiar cell in Tom Dwight's jail.

Chapter 25

"Do you rent horses, friend?"

"Does a bear shit in the woods?"

"Probably. But d'you rent horses?" Longarm repeated.

The gent at the livery grunted. "I don't know you."

"No, sir, you don't. Allow me to introduce myself. I'm the fellow who keeps wanting to know d'you rent out horses."

"To strangers?"

"To anybody."

"You want to rent one for yourself, do you?"

"Mister, it's a simple enough thing I'm asking you. Now do you rent horses or don't you?"

"There's no need for you to get testy about it. Of course I rents horses. Rents horses and sells feeds. That's what I do for a living."

"Fine. I want to rent a horse."

"Saddle too?"

"With a saddle. And bridle. And shoes on its feet. All that shit."

"Dollar a day. In advance."

"I'll give you a government voucher."

"You can do that if you like, but you won't be getting

125

no horse if you do. Cash on the barrelhead or it's no deal."

Longarm grumbled. But he reached into his pocket for the dollar. Cash. On the damn barrelhead.

Longarm's stomach was growling by the time he got to the Hendrikson farm. He rode in slowly and stopped in the farmyard. He could not see anyone on the place, but the chickens were wandering free around the house, scratching for bugs or seeds or whatever they could find. A pair of fat sows were lying in a patch of shade with some pigs pulling at their teats. The farm looked tidy and reasonably prosperous.

The aroma of freshly baked bread drifted out of an open window, and he thought he could hear the muted clatter of dishes and tableware. He reined a little closer to the porch and called, "Hello. Is anybody home?"

A young woman with a towel in her hands appeared in the doorway. She was blond and a little on the chubby side. She wore her hair in pigtails, which made her look even younger than she undoubtedly was. Undoubtedly, he thought, because of the size of her tits. She had a chest that preceded her by a good foot and a half . . . or so it seemed at first glance anyway.

Longarm swiftly removed his hat. "Afternoon, miss."

"Good day to you, mister. What can I do for you?"

"I'm hungry, miss, an' I was hoping I could get a bite o' lunch from you. I'd be willin' to pay. I'm not asking for no handout."

The girl tilted her head and examined him for a moment, then said, "Fif . . . uh, twenty-five cents. Can you pay that much?"

"Yes, miss. Twenty-five." He dipped into his pocket and brought out a handful of small change, sorted through it, and counted out a dime and three nickels.

"Step down then." The girl took the coins from him

before she said, "My papa isn't here right now and it wouldn't look right for you to come inside the house with me here alone. Do you go into the barn there, I'll bring a sandwich out to you and a cup of fresh buttermilk. Maybe some buttered bread warm from the oven."

Longarm smiled. "Did you bake the bread yourself?"

"Yes, I did."

"Then I know it will be tasty. Anything that comes from a girl as fine-looking as you is bound t' be good."

"Why, sir . . . how you do flatter a girl."

"No more than you deserve."

"You can tie your horse over yonder then and I'll meet you in the barn."

Longarm's smile flashed again. "Don't be long, y'hear?"

The girl turned and went back inside the house. Longarm led his rented horse in the direction the girl had indicated.

Chapter 26

The lunch she brought out to him was good enough. Hot bread with fresh butter melted over it, chunks of bacon contained in biscuits that had been split and smeared with bacon grease from the frying, and a large mug of buttermilk, which suggested that they had cattle somewhere on the farm as well as the critters Longarm had already seen. Horses too, more than likely. Those would be needed to handle the plowing and the farm wagon.

The girl delivered the food on a tray, then excused herself and returned to the house saying she had to finish her washing.

For a little while there, Longarm thought he just might have misjudged this whole situation.

Then the girl came back.

"You're a awful handsome gentleman," she shyly said, making circles in the dirt with the toe of her shoe.

"Now that's mighty kind of you," Longarm said. "Thank you. And if I may say so, you're a very pretty girl." That was not quite true, but he'd never yet met a girl who did not want to receive a compliment. And hell, it was close enough.

"Mister, you look just good enough to eat."

129

Longarm said nothing, just waited.

"In fact, mister, I look at you and I think, wow, I'd like to taste that fine gentleman's dick. You know?"

"I, uh . . . just like that?"

"Well, I'd sure like to. And I would do it. I'd drop right down and suck your dick, mister"—she paused for a second—"if you would make me the loan of a dollar, that is."

"Loan?"

She giggled. "We could call it that. So's you wouldn't be thinking of me like some common whore or sum'thin'." She kept her eyes down, kept swinging her toe in the straw and dirt and chicken litter on the floor.

"What if I don't have a whole dollar left?"

"I seen that pocket full of change you're carrying. All those coins 'ud just cause a lump in your britches and weigh you down."

"Yes?"

"How's about you pay me that money. Loan it to me, I mean. Won't either one of us have to count it. I'll call it enough if you will."

"And if it's more than a dollar?"

She giggled again and broke into a big smile, looking up to lock her eyes with his. "Then this is my lucky day. And yours too, mister. So what do you say? Do you want me to suck your dick? To, um, sort of relax you. After lunch, if you see what I mean."

"A man can always use some relaxation," Longarm said. He reached into his pocket, dug deep, and pulled out the entire handful of small change. It was all nickel and silver with no yellow metal mixed in. He was sure of that, although the girl was probably hoping for a tiny golden windfall. She was surely going to be disappointed.

The busty little blonde laughed happily as she cupped her hands to accept the spill of coins. She transferred them to the pocket of her apron and dropped to her knees, hiking her skirts up a little so she would not soil the cloth.

The girl's fingers flew, slipping free the buttons at Longarm's crotch and reaching inside to find and pull out his pecker.

Up until then he had been more interested in what was going on around him than in the thought of this girl's warm, moist mouth. His pecker came out soft and flaccid and lay on the palm of her hand like a small newborn animal of some sort.

That changed.

The feel of her hand on him and the warmth of her breath against his flesh brought an inevitable response, and the blind snake began to sit up and pay attention.

It was a funny thing, but that little farm girl was an awful lot prettier down on her knees with his cock in her hand than she had been when she was standing upright.

She leaned forward a bit and experimentally licked the tip of his cock. That did it. It sprang to attention, as ramrod straight as any fancy cavalry officer's back. And when she peeled the foreskin back and ran her tongue around the purple bulb, Longarm saluted. More or less.

He braced his legs a little apart and felt the heat of being inside the blonde's mouth.

"Whoo-whee!" he muttered.

The girl did not answer, but he could feel her laughter. She cupped his balls on the palm of one hand and with the other took a firm hold on his shaft, then commenced to bobbing her head up and down.

Damn, but that felt good.

The girl made wet, gobbling sounds as she sucked. Longarm could feel the swelling rise of sap gathering somewhere deep in his balls and demanding to be released.

He was going to . . .

Well, shit!

He looked toward the side of the barn and saw a gray-haired old man standing there with a pitchfork in his hands and a look of fury on his bearded face.

Even so, Longarm had already passed the point of no return.

The old man spoke. The girl pulled away. And Longarm came.

Milky jism shot out of his cock and jetted into the girl's eyes, painting her face and running down her cheeks to drip off her chin.

She squealed.

The old man bellowed.

And Custis Long permitted himself a very small smile.

Chapter 27

"He made me do it, Daddy, he forced me, he said he'd shoot me if I didn't take that awful thing in my mouth, Daddy. I didn't want to touch him, Daddy, but he made me, he did, Daddy, it was terrible, I was so awful scared. Daddy, help me, Daddy, help me."

The girl bounced to her feet and ran blubbering to her father, her words all running together so that Longarm marveled she was able to get it all out without seeming to draw breath. She dropped to her knees and hugged her father's legs, burying her face against the rough cloth of his overalls and sobbing. And, Longarm noticed, using that pathetic appeal to smear some of Longarm's cum off her face and onto her father's overalls.

Hell, Longarm almost believed her himself, it was that good a performance.

The farmer was babbling something too, although Longarm was only halfway bothering to pay attention. He was yammering something about "innocent baby" and "call the law on you" and "ruined forever" and "you could be hanged from an old oak tree" and more shit of that nature.

The man brandished his pitchfork and made his

threats. Which, when you thought about it, was an amazingly stupid and dangerous thing for him to do since he could plainly see that this stranger whose cock the girl just sucked was armed with a large-caliber revolver.

A man of criminal bent, or simply one who would go beyond his normal limits in order to avoid a rope or a long prison term, might not be all that frightened of an old man with a pitchfork. Not when two bullets from his belly gun would dispatch the farmer and the girl too. Four cents worth of cartridges against twenty-five years in prison? The farmer was definitely treading dangerous ground here, assuming a very large degree of decency in the strangers he was trying to blackmail.

And Longarm had no doubt whatsoever that this was a game the gent and daughter had played more than once in the past. They knew what they were doing and as long as they were not challenged too often, they would continue to get away with it undetected.

Well, those days were coming to an end, Longarm figured.

"Don't tell the sheriff," Longarm said, picking up his end of things. "It was all her idea. I never suggested any such thing, but she said she'd do me if I paid her a dollar. Just please don't tell the sheriff. I'll do . . . I'll do most anything to avoid that. Please!"

The farmer and his daughter both calmed themselves with amazing speed once Longarm started talking along those lines.

The man lowered the tines of his menacing pitchfork and cleared his throat as if in deep thought. "Well, we might see our way clear to keep this between ourselves. You know. If, um, if we had a good reason. I mean, I wouldn't want the whole county knowing what you done to my little girl, shaming her like that. There wouldn't be any boy would want to marry her if he knew she'd had to suffer what you done to her. It could ruin her reputation."

Longarm stood where he was.

A puff of cool breeze swept through the barn and he felt a very small and localized chill that reminded him his prick was still dangling out of his fly. He reached down and put it back where it belonged, then took his time buttoning his trousers. Neither the farmer nor the girl offered any reaction, and Longarm was damned if he would turn away from them. Let them watch. He really didn't much care.

The farmer paused, and Longarm got the impression he was expecting this stranger to say something. To offer some reason exactly *why* the man should not call in the law.

When Longarm failed to make a suggestion, the farmer had to do it himself. He cleared his throat again and said, "I suppose, thinking about it, I suppose we'uns could be persuaded to keep this just between ourselves."

"Persuaded?"

The girl grabbed her father's elbow. "Daddy, he raped me. I was so awful scared. I don't know if I will ever be able to be a proper wife when someday I marry. I guess this man has ruined me, Daddy. Don't let him just ride off and leave me here."

"You could give the child a little something to ease her mind," the farmer suggested.

"What sort of a little something would you have in mind?"

"Oh, I don't know. Maybe a little money. So she could buy herself something pretty. You know what store girls set on being able to shop. That might make her feel better."

"I already paid her a dollar," Longarm said. "She can shop with that."

135

"A dollar? A single damn dollar for ruining her life forever? You ain't gonna be let off that cheap, mister. Don't you forget, I can always just tell the sheriff that you raped my little girl. All it takes is one word from an upstanding citizen like me and you'll find yourself behind bars, stranger." He snorted and shook his pitchfork. "Just one word."

"If not the dollar, then what?" Longarm asked.

"Oh, I'm thinking . . . say . . . fifty dollars."

"Fifty dollars? For one blow job that I could get in town for fifty cents?"

"Mind your language around my baby," the farmer warned.

"If she's old enough to suck cock, she's old enough to hear it talked about," Longarm returned. "And I'm not paying you no damn fifty dollars for that blow job. Besides, you came in and interrupted me. I didn't get to squirt inside her mouth. T' my mind that makes for a piss-poor blow job and I'm not paying no fifty dollars for it. I wouldn't pay her fifty dollars even if she came back now and gobbled it again so's she could swallow it like she should ought to 've done to begin with."

"Jesus God, mister, you got a nerve on you."

"Yeah, maybe so. Fact remains, I'm not paying you no damn fifty dollars."

"All right. Twenty then."

"Twenty dollars?"

"That's right. Twenty dollars cash money or I hitch up old Belvedere and drive to town for the sheriff right this very minute."

"You say you are threatening me with a claim of rape if I don't pay you twenty dollars," Longarm said.

"That's it exactly. Twenty dollars cash or me and her go find Sheriff Tom Dwight. If we do that, he'll have you behind bars before nightfall."

"All right. You've spelled it out clear enough. I reckon I got no choice about this."

"No, sir, you damn sure do not. Now pay up."

Longarm shrugged.

He reached inside his coat and produced his wallet. The girl hugged her daddy's elbow and rose onto tip-toes, practically giddy with the thought of all the money that was coming their way. The father gave Longarm a smug, self-satisfied look.

That look froze and turned into one of consternation when Longarm flipped his wallet open to display not a sheaf of folding currency but a badge.

"You, sir, are under arrest," Longarm said firmly, "on charges of extortion, intimidation, threatening a federal peace officer. . . . I'll set down with the United States attorney for this district an' see what-all other charges him and me can come up with.

"In the meantime, sir, you will be incarcerated in jail until such time as I can transport you for an appearance before a federal court. Now set that pitchfork aside an' turn around, please, so's I can put the handcuffs on you."

"But . . . but . . ."

"Little girl, you ain't under arrest so you can do whatever you like."

"Daddy?"

"Jesus!" the farmer blurted.

"Mister? Mister? Let my daddy go. I could suck you again. Real good this time. Or I could fuck you extra good."

"Careful, missy, or you'll find yourself in cuffs too for attempting to bribe a deputy United States marshal. Mister, you'd best be turning around and putting your hands back where I can get to them. And do it quick before I get the idea that you're resisting arrest. Do it *now*!"

Chapter 28

"So you see, Sheriff sir, the whole thing was my fault, sir, because I was so scared, you see, what with my daddy walking up on us, and I said things that weren't true, so as to keep Daddy from whupping me, and I am just terrible sorry, sir, and I hope you'll forgive me and if you can see it clear in your heart, I hope you won't be telling it around what I done, but it was my idea and he's such a nice man and I wanted some money to shop with, and he paid me a whole dollar, just like he said he done when he was on trial, and I lied then but it was my fault and he didn't do no wrong, and then Mr. Marshal Long came and talked to me and convinced me that the best thing for ever'body is for me to tell the truth while I still can without sending Mr. Handley off to prison, so I hope . . . Sheriff, sir, I hope we can just kind of forget the whole thing." She tilted her head and gave Tom Dwight a smile so sweet that you knew butter wouldn't melt in her mouth.

Longarm was impressed. Not by the confession. She had agreed to that in exchange for keeping her daddy out of jail. What impressed him all to hell and gone was how many words Letty Hendrikson could get out of her mouth without stopping to breathe. The girl likely practiced that by holding her breath while she sucked cock, he realized. The truth was that Longarm did not like this girl overmuch, never mind that she gave a pretty decent blow job.

"All right, honey, we'll . . . uh . . . we'll find a way to work this out. Thank you for telling me." Dwight shifted his attention to the girl's father. "I expect you can go now, Cal, but mind you keep an eye on this girl's upbringing from here on. She's more than old enough to know better. Hell, Cal, marry her off to somebody before the word gets out. It's either that or expect her to wind up in a crib somewhere. Count on it."

"Yes, sir, I will do that," the farmer said humbly. "Can we go now?" He gathered his hat in his hands and hiked his overalls a little higher.

"Yes," the sheriff said.

"No," Longarm countered.

Both men and the girl stopped and looked at Longarm.

"You boys are forgettin' that two horses, a wagon, an' the contents of that outfit was confiscated from John Handley. I believe you have all that stuff, Hendrikson. Return it. All of it. You have until break of day tomorrow."

"I forgot about that," the farmer said with such feeling that Longarm knew good and well the man was lying.

"Bullshit!"

"I can't . . . I'll have to gather it all up. I don't know what's become of it all."

"Bullshit," Longarm repeated. "Dawn tomorrow."

"I can't possibly . . ."

"It's either that or a prison term. D'you want me to fill the sheriff in on the particulars so's we can start processing you now? Or will you wait to tomorrow? And don't for a minute think you can run anyplace that I can't find you. I can. I would. An' I'll add a charge of evading a law enforcement officer if I have t' do that."

"I, uh, perhaps I can . . ."

"You can. And the outfit damn sure better be complete. You and that girl of yours ain't entitled to so much as a horseshoe nail out of Handley's stuff, so make sure it's here every bit."

Hendrikson and his girl did not look happy. That was fine by Longarm. If they came out of this deal happy, then he was doing something wrong.

"I forgot about that myself," Dwight said when the Hendriksons were gone. "Glad you remembered."

Longarm sighed and helped himself to a seat in front of the sheriff's desk. He reached for a cheroot, nipped the tip off with his teeth, and spit the bit of twisted tobacco toward the spittoon. He missed. "Cigar?" he offered.

"No, thanks."

Longarm grunted and dipped two fingers inside his vest pocket to produce a match. He took his time about getting the cheroot lighted and a good coal started.

"What will we do with Handley?" Dwight asked. "Should I release him now?"

"Nope." Longarm looked for a place to prop his feet up, failed to find anything, and resigned himself to sitting upright instead. "He's still wanted in Colorado on the warrant that brought me here t' begin with. It was just his lucky day that the girl happened t' confess to me what she done. But that only drops your charges. Which I trust you an' your judge will work out somehow. Me, I'm concerned with those charges back in Colorado. The man stays behind bars, Sheriff, until those are resolved."

"If that is your judgment on the matter, that's what we will do."

141

Longarm nodded. "Seeing as I'm responsible for him, I'll fetch supper to him tonight. The county shouldn't ought to pay for that."

"I appreciate that," Dwight said.

Longarm stood. "If you will excuse me, Sheriff, I'm a mite hungry my own self. I'm gonna go get something to eat. I'll bring a basket back for Handley later on this evenin'."

When he walked out onto the Edwardsville streets, Longarm was feeling pretty good about the way this was turning out.

Now all he had to do was figure out why Jack Handley was so damned reticent when it came to discussing that shooting in Manitou. And what, if anything, he could do about it.

Chapter 29

Longarm had a moment of nervousness when he approached the boardinghouse. After all, the last time he was here Mrs. Pettijohn had his cum on her breath. It had been fine at the time, but it was not an experience he would want to repeat in daylight.

He need not have worried. The big woman acted like he was just another returning customer, reminded him of which room would be his, and fed him. There was not a hint of anything else in her voice or her movements, for which Longarm was supremely glad. Nice as she had been to him before, and as much as he had needed it, he did not want any repeat of the experience.

He slept lightly that night, halfway expecting Hilda Pettijohn to again come to him in the night, but morning found him still alone. Alone and—proving the perversity of humankind—perhaps just a little disappointed that she had *not* sought his bed in the night.

Longarm chuckled a little that morning when he peered into the mirror for his shave. But what the hell. Man or woman, young or old, we get along the best we can. And that goes for deputy United States marshals too.

"Thank you, Mrs. Pettijohn," he said after breakfast as he was about to leave. "For everything."

"Come again, Mr. Long. You are always welcome here."

"I'll leave your basket with the sheriff if that's all right." He had Jack Handley's breakfast in a basket hanging on his arm.

"That will be fine, thank you."

He was about halfway tempted to give the lady a good-bye kiss, but they were standing on her front porch in full view of anyone who happened to look in that direction. It would not have been a seemly display out in public like that, and he certainly did not want to do anything that would sully her reputation. After all, she had to live here while he would be moving on . . . just as quickly as he could.

Longarm grunted with satisfaction when he walked around behind the courthouse to reach the jail. It was only a half hour or forty-five minutes past daybreak, but that son of a bitch Hendrikson already had Jack's wagon parked there.

At least Longarm assumed the mud wagon with canvas sides drawn by a pair of fancy-colored paint horses belonged to Jack Handley. Longarm untied one edge of the dust curtain in back and peeped inside. He could not know what Handley had had in there to begin with, but certainly the wagon was fully loaded now, set up not unlike a sheepherder wagon with built-in storage bins, a cot, and what looked to be a normal complement of personal possessions. Obviously, Hendrikson had understood that the deputy was damned well serious when he warned the farmer to surrender everything that did not properly belong to him. It looked like he had done exactly that.

Longarm took the breakfast basket inside—Dwight was not in his office and the door was locked so Long-

arm had to use the "hidden" key again to gain entry—
then went out to finish their preparations so he and his
prisoner could get the hell out of Edwardsville.

He unhitched Jack's paint horses and took them
around, still in harness, to hook them on to his prison
wagon. Then he removed the tongue from Jack's mud
wagon and shoved it tight against the tailgate of the
prison wagon.

He chained the doubletree of the mud wagon to the
back of the prison wagon so the two were joined much
like a wagon and trailer.

He got his own team from the shed where he'd left
them overnight and fitted their harnesses to them, then
led them into position in front of Jack's team and
hooked the traces of his pair so the two pairs of horses
could pull the wagons as a four-up.

The driving lines were a little short for comfort, but
were long enough. Just barely, but then barely enough is
indeed enough.

By the time Longarm had the rig ready, Jack was finished with his meal and all that remained was to wait for
Tom Dwight to return from wherever the man had gotten off to.

"I could open the cell door for you if you are in a
hurry," Handley offered.

"Thanks but I don't want spook the sheriff. It might
could disconcert him t' find out the violent prisoner he's
been so careful to keep under lock an' key has had the
run of the damn place this whole time."

The chubby, cherubic prisoner grinned. "Whatever
you say."

"Besides," Longarm said, "we got us a long way t'
go. There's no need wearin' ourselves and those horses
out tryin' to do it all in a day. We'll take whatever time
we need. An' Jack . . ."

"Yes?"

145

"Before we get back t' Manitou you are gonna have to come clean with me about a few things. Starting with whatever beef it was you had with that postal clerk Ed Marsh that you went an' killed."

"Whatever you think best, Custis." Handley grinned. "I mean Longarm."

"Yes, sir. We got plenty of time for you t' talk and me to listen, and I figure to use it."

Chapter 30

The two pairs of horses were not accustomed to pulling as one team. They were balky and fractious, and it pissed Longarm off to try to drive an unruly team, especially with those short reins. As soon as they were well clear of Edwardsville he stopped, disconnected the wagons, and hitched the two separate pairs where they rightly belonged on two separate rigs.

"You aren't turning me loose, are you?" Handley asked with an undertone of hope in his voice.

"Not damn likely. The law is the law an' I'm bounden to uphold it, but that don't mean I got to be miserable while I'm doin' it. Like for instance trying t' drive these flea-bit sons o' bitches. I figure t' accept your parole an' let you drive your own damn rig. It'll be a whole lot more comfortable for both of us than me fighting with these nags an' you bouncing around inside that cage."

"I have not offered my parole," Handley pointed out.

"But you're going to, right?"

Handley took his time about answering, first feigning deep thought as he rubbed his forehead and made pained faces. After a few moments, he brightened and nodded. "All right. You have my parole. I will not try to slip away. Although come to think of it, I am positive that my fine lads here could outrun those . . . whatever they are . . . that are pulling your wagon. It could be that I spoke too soon for my own good."

"The good of it," Longarm said, "is that they can't hang you but once."

"You don't think . . ."

Longarm shrugged. "That ain't up to me, Jack. My job is to get you there so's you can stand trial. Whatever happens after that is up t' the judge an' a jury."

Handley gave him a long look, finally taking a deep breath and sighing. "Perhaps I was too quick to give that parole."

"Maybe, but now that you done it, you'll stick by it."

"Do you think so?"

"I know so. You're an honorable man, Jack. I got no doubt about that."

"Honor can be a heavy burden to carry," Handley said.

"Have you done any traveling over in the Indian Nations, Jack?"

"Not much. Why do you ask?"

"They got their own way of doin' things, those Five Civilized Tribes. I know 'cause I've worked over there from time to time, riding for Parker's court. It spooked me at first how they deal with their convicted murderers. Men who've been convicted an' sentenced to hang can give their parole an' go home."

"You are serious about that?"

"Aye, so I am. If they give their word that they'll come back, they are given time enough to go home . . . unsupervised, mind you . . . so they can get a last crop in an' see to their wives an' kids an' make their peace with whatever gods they worship. Then comes the date for the hanging, they go an' surrender themselves. They ain't like us, Jack, but they sure as hell know what honor means."

"I am humbled, Longarm. I want to learn more about these native peoples, I think. Perhaps study them. In any event, you already have my word of honor. I'll not go back on it."

"I know you won't, Jack. Now rustle us up a little firewood, would you? I'm hankering a cup o' coffee to hold me till suppertime."

Handley grinned. "Now I understand. You didn't want me to handle my wagon so much as you wanted a camp swamper to do the hard chores."

"That's right. I figure t' lie in the shade an' watch while you do all the hard work, Jack, all the way back to Manitou."

The drive back to Denver was painful for Longarm. On the drive out he had had Emily seated beside him, so perky and pretty and dear. Now she lay under the sod with not even any family left to mourn her nor any of her people buried close beside her. Longarm's mood was melancholy, and he supposed he was poor company when they took a break for meals or to overnight.

"We're gonna go through Denver to get down t' Manitou," Longarm said one evening as he and Jack Handley took their coffee and sat upwind of the fire to avoid getting smoke in their eyes . . . an exercise that Longarm knew good and well was futile. Sometimes, he could swear that smoke is attracted to people's eyes so strongly that it will sneak into the breeze in order to pester a man. However, an evening fire is a comfort in spite of that.

"Isn't that the long way around?" Handley asked.

"Sure it is, but I wanta turn this prison wagon in an' get a saddle horse. Figure to tie it onto the back o' your rig an' ride the rest o' the way with you. That'll be more sensible . . . an' a damn sight more comfortable . . . than us takin' the two wagons all that way. Besides, there's some shit I gotta do in Denver that I'd just as soon get outa the way."

"I take it the young lady had relatives there?" Handley asked.

Longarm shook his head and reached inside his coat for a cigar. "No. Just friends. She was part of a theater troupe. Emily was their ingenue. They'll be counting on her. Best they should know what happened that she can't be there with them."

"All right." The fat little man grinned. "It isn't like I am in any hurry to reach Manitou."

"I kinda figured that. An' I sorta hate to tell you, but when we get there I'll have t' put you in the jail overnight while I do the things I got to do." Longarm smiled at this chubby fellow who seemed more friend than prisoner. "In case you haven't noticed, Jack, I'm commencing to smell a mite ripe. 'Mong other things, I wanta stop at home an' change these clothes for something that don't smell like horse sweat an' campfire smoke."

"Then if you don't mind, I will do a little laundry myself before we make the last push down to Denver."

"Fair enough," Longarm told him. "We can lay over a day if you need."

"I would like that." Handley looked up toward the stars and sighed. "Freedom is a hard thing to give up, Longarm."

"Yes, I . . ."

Longarm never finished the sentence. When he glanced in Jack Handley's direction, he saw that the St. Nicholas lookalike had a large-caliber derringer in his hand.

The fat man shrugged and again sighed. He turned

the tiny pistol around so the butt, not the muzzle, was pointing in Longarm's direction. "Keep this for me, would you, please? It probably would not be a good idea for the warders to find this on me when you take me to the jail."

"Jesus, Jack. You did give me a start there." Longarm accepted the little gun and dropped it into his pocket. "Have you had that on you all along?"

Handley grinned and nodded.

"Dammit, Jack, before we get down to Manitou, you an' me got to do some serious talking about what-all you done to put you in this predicament."

"Whatever you say, friend Longarm."

They laid over at the campsite an entire extra day while Jack Handley washed clothes and put his wagon in order.

And Handley talked—openly and with apparent honesty—much of the time they were there.

Chapter 31

Longarm liked Manitou. Always had. He always felt a surge of pleasure when he put Colorado City with its cardsharps and rigged gaming tables behind him and made that last little leg beside a cold-water creek to Manitou, lying there at the foot of Ute Pass like some sort of gateway into the mountains.

Many a time he had ridden through, and the pretty little town never ceased to please him.

Longarm inclined his head to the right as they reached the outskirts of town and said, "There's springs over there. They was sacred to the Indians. That's where they got the name o' the place. Manitou, the Great Spirit. They thought he lived there at the springs. Nowadays, they let tourists come an' drink a little cup o' the water, but they charge a fee for it. Did you try it when you was here before?"

"Yes." Handley made a sour face, his mouth and eyes and everything collapsing around his nose.

Longarm laughed. "Yeah. Tastes like shit, don't it." Then Longarm became serious. "Jack, we're here now. I'd best be putting the handcuffs on you. Sorry."

"Oh, I understand. There will be no hard feelings regardless of what happens." The chubby man turned on the wagon seat and held his wrists out so Longarm could more easily clamp the steel on him.

Longarm put them on loosely so they would not bind. Not that it mattered. He knew good and well if Jack wanted out of the cuffs, he could open them without a key almost as quickly as Longarm could unlatch them with his key.

"Look at that," Handley said, holding his wrists up and feigning amazement. "A perfect fit."

"Will you quit showin' your jewelry off? Folks are looking. Now try an' be good, will you? For a change."

Handley chuckled. But he settled back in the seat and let Longarm do the driving.

Longarm brought them to a halt in front of the town's jail, an aging structure built of stone, logs, and mud. The roof had been patched many a time, and there was a good amount of rot in the ground-level pine logs. The place looked like it must have been one of the earliest buildings erected in the town, and might have started out as someone's home. Now it housed the town's three-man police force and two small, iron-barred cells.

"Welcome home, Jack."

"Thank you just ever so much," Handley said, sarcasm thick in his voice.

"It's the least I could do for a friend." Longarm set the brake and wrapped the lines around the whip socket, then hopped down and clipped a hitching weight to the bit of the fancy paint horse on the nigh side of the hitch.

"Stay there," he cautioned when Handley shifted over to the side of the driving box. "I don't want you falling out an' breaking your neck."

"Isn't a broken neck what happens when a person is hanged?" Handley said. "That is right, isn't it? The actual cause of death is a broken neck."

"Yeah, Jack. That's right." Longarm came back to the side of the wagon and took hold of Handley's arm to help the fat man climb down to the street, then led him inside the ramshackle police station.

Longarm did not know the young constable who was sitting at the only desk in the place, the chair swiveled sideways and his feet propped on an overturned wastebasket. He needed a repair to the sole of his right shoe as a hole was wearing thin and would soon be all the way through.

"Is Chief Anderson around?" Longarm asked.

The constable looked up and gave both visitors a sullen look. "Who wants to know?"

"I do, dammit. An' I asked you a perfectly civil question. I figure the least you can do is t' give me an answer."

"Go fuck yourself."

Longarm swung his boot, kicking the wastebasket out from under the constable's feet. Smartass little son of a bitch. Probably, Longarm thought, one of those self-important assholes who think once they pin a badge to their chests that all of a sudden their shit don't stink.

The constable surged to his feet, his hand grabbing for the butt of a revolver at his belt.

Longarm was quicker. He yanked the constable's pistol out and tossed it onto the desk while with his other hand he took a firm grip on the red-haired young man's throat. "Sonny, I eat kids like you for breakfast. Now settle yourself down an' tell me where I can find Jim Anderson. Better yet, you can run find him for me. You can tell him that Deputy United States

Marshal Custis Long is here with a prisoner Jim has paper on."

"Long . . . Longarm? You are Longarm? Really?"

"It's Deputy Long to you, kid. My friends call me Longarm an' so do some o' my enemies. But you ain't neither of those. Unless you want t' make yourself an enemy. I think maybe we could arrange that."

"I . . . I'm sorry, sir. Really. I didn't know. I'm sorry I smarted off to you. Yes, sir. I'll go get the chief. Right away. I'll tell him you are here."

"Fine." Longarm turned. "Which cell d'you prefer, Jack?"

"That one, I think," Handley said, pointing.

"Fine. It's yours." Longarm unlocked the handcuffs—he most certainly did not want this young constable to see how easily Jack could manipulate locks—and put them back into his pocket.

Handley went into the chosen cell, tested the tension on the ropes holding the mattress on the cell's cot, and pronounced himself satisfied. "This will do."

Longarm swung the door shut and clipped the padlock into place on it. For whatever that was worth.

By the time he looked around, the constable was gone leaving the front door standing open.

"I'm not sure, Longarm, but I think the boy came close to wetting himself."

"He came close to worse'n that," Longarm growled. He had been in a good humor when he got here, but the damned kid took care of that.

"Yes?"

"Now that we're here, keep your mouth shut, will you?"

"What about the police chief? Surely I can talk to him."

"Not to him, not to nobody. Is that clear? You don't say shit. An' you don't ask for anything neither. I'll see to your grub and whatever else needs t' be done. Are we clear about this? It's important, Jack. Trust me."

Handley paused only for a moment before he nodded and solemnly said, "That I do, friend Longarm. That I surely do."

Chapter 32

Chief of Police James Anderson was a man of medium height and carefully trimmed hair. Longarm had never seen the man needing a shave. He was always tidy, even meticulous, about his clothing and grooming. He was, however, a man who had been up the trail and over the mountains. Longarm thought him too much the dandy, but nonetheless respected him. Did not necessarily like Anderson or consider him to be a friend, but he did know and respect the Manitou chief.

"What do you have for us today, Longarm?" Anderson asked immediately upon coming inside. He did not bother with greetings and there was interest but no warmth in his voice. The red-haired constable was close on the chief's heels.

Longarm offered his hand to shake before he answered. "I believe you got paper out on a fella named John Handley, Jim. Wanted for the murder of a postal clerk?"

"Yes, we do."

"Well, he's setting in that cell yonder. Found him up in Dakota Territory."

"Headed for the border, no doubt."

Longarm shrugged. He had never asked Jack where he was going when he ran into that trouble at Edwardsville.

"Thank you for your help, Longarm. I will prepare the paperwork on your man. Can you come back this afternoon to sign off on it and collect your copies?"

"That's not a problem. But I would like t' ask you some questions about the, uh, incident. T' get it all straight in my mind, you might say."

"Oh? Why would that be?"

"I got reports t' do too, Jim. When I get back t' Denver I'll be writing out reports till my fingers cramp up an' turn into knots."

"Yes, of course you would have your own reports to make. It would be a help to me if you could ask Marshal Vail to have a copy made for me."

That request would thoroughly piss off Henry. As Billy Vail's clerk, any such instruction would mean he would have to hand-copy whatever Longarm put down. That, however, would lie somewhere between brief and nonexistent. Longarm did not much hold with wasting time writing shit down on paper.

All Longarm could do now, though, was to nod and agree. "I'll ask him."

"Thank you."

"I been on the road for a good spell, Jim. D'you think we could go get some coffee or somethin' while we talk?"

"Certainly. Gary, make sure the prisoner has bedding, drinking water, and a clean bucket. Then you can make the rounds through the alleys, please."

"Yes, sir."

"This way, Longarm. We have a café in town that I believe opened for business after the last time you were here. They have the best pies I have ever tasted."

"Pie sounds good, Jim."

And it was. It was excellent, in fact, as was the coffee. Longarm intended to remember this place and come again, at least so long as it lasted. In these smaller towns like Manitou, small businesses went in and out of existence almost as often as a squirrel will go in and out of its den, or so it sometimes seemed. When Longarm returned to a place, even one he knew well, he could never be sure of who or what he would find. He hoped this café would become a permanent part of the Manitou landscape. Hell, he hoped the proprietor would sell out here and move to Denver.

Longarm quickly finished off a quarter of a huckleberry pie, accepted a refill of his coffee, and settled back with his legs extended and boots crossed at the ankles. He offered Anderson a cigar and took care of trimming and lighting his own cheroot before he got down to the business at hand.

"Jim, I'd like to know what-all happened here when Ed Marsh was shot."

"It was a simple enough case of murder, Longarm. A straightforward shooting. I gather there was no bad blood between Handley and Marsh."

"Handley was just passing through, wasn't he?"

"He had been here for a few days when it happened. Three or four, I think."

"But he was essentially a stranger in town whereas Marsh lived here."

"That's right."

"Was Marsh popular?" Longarm asked.

"He was . . . people here were accustomed to him. And there was an element with whom he was friendly."

"In other words, he could be a sonuvabitch but he had his pack o' cronies?"

"Something like that."

Longarm had a swallow of the excellent coffee and set the mug back down. "What d'you know about the shooting, Jim?"

"The person you should be talking with is my constable, Gary Cole. He is the one who investigated the murder and made out the reports."

"I'll do that too, o' course, and I'd like t' read your reports on the matter."

"Fine. We can do that as soon as we get back to the office. You have already met young Cole."

"He's the redheaded kid?"

"Yes. He is my nephew. Sort of."

"How does a person be 'sort of' kin?" Longarm breathed out a smoke ring, then smiled at the way it hung in the air for several long moments before the waiter's passage distorted one side and finally the white ring faded out of sight until it disappeared completely.

"Eight years ago my brother Kenneth married young Gary's mother. She was a widow lady living in Fairplay. The boy's father was killed in a mining accident."

"Rough." Longarm finished his coffee. "I didn't know you have a brother, Jim."

"I have four brothers and a baby sister."

Longarm found himself wondering if the sister was as fussy and tidy as her older brother. Not that he ever expected to find out. And not that it mattered anyway. But for a moment he found himself visualizing someone with Jim Anderson's stern and chiseled features but with long hair. And tits. He made a face and looked away.

"Are you done?" the police chief asked.

"Yeah, I'm ready."

"Then I suggest we go back to my office so you can read young Cole's reports. You can interview him when he returns from walking the rounds."

Longarm nodded.

Anderson took out a coin purse and very carefully sorted out exact change for their pie and coffee. He placed it on the table. He did not leave a tip.

When Anderson turned to leave the café, Longarm

hung back for a moment so he could place a tip beside his empty cup. Waiters and waitresses are on their feet, running all day to take care of customers, and they do it for damned little pay. The way Longarm saw it they more than earned the tips they collected in the course of their work.

"Are you coming, Longarm?"

"Right behind you, Jim."

Chapter 33

"Jim, where can I find this . . . uh . . . Harold Joyner?" Longarm asked, peering at one of a thick sheaf of papers in his hand.

"Joyner is the swamper at Phil Coburn's bowling alley," the police chief said.

"Bowling alley?" Longarm's eyebrows went up.

"Duckpins," Anderson explained. "It's a popular place. A man can get a drink there, and on weekends the bar is closed and the ladies and kids are welcome. It is in the next block, second floor over the pharmacy."

"Thanks." Longarm stood and stretched, then placed the papers—the police reports about the shooting of Edwin Theodore Marsh—on the corner of Jim Anderson's desk. "Think I'll go stretch my legs for a few minutes. I'll finish going over these when I get back."

"I will tell Gary to wait for you if he returns before you do."

Longarm thanked the man again and fetched his brown Stetson from a wall peg. Once outside, he paused to light a smoke and look up and down the street to make sure he knew which direction the pharmacy was in. Then he strode briskly along, his boot heels coming down hard on the sidewalk boards.

A steep flight of stairs led up the east wall outside the pharmacy. A very small, professionally painted sign pointed the way to the bowling alley. Longarm hustled up to the second floor. The door was open and he was greeted with the aroma of pipe smoke and floor wax.

There were three of the narrow duckpin alleys. Only one was in use at this early afternoon time of day, but there were benches where a handful of idlers were watching a match between two gentlemen in shirtsleeves.

"Care to roll a few?" a heavyset gent asked with a smile. Longarm assumed he would be Coburn the proprietor.

"Thanks, but I'm here looking for Harold Joyner."

"May I ask what business you have with him?" Coburn's initial friendliness had iced over and turned to caution.

"I like a man who tries t' take care of his friends. I admire that," Longarm said. He flipped his wallet open to display the badge there and quickly added, "Your man ain't in any sort of trouble. He was witness to a shooting a while back. I wanta ask him about that is all."

Coburn looked puzzled. Then he shrugged and turned his head. "Shorty. Come here, please."

A small man in clean but much-worn clothing got up from one of the benches and joined them. "Yes, sir?"

"How come you never told me you witnessed a shooting, Shorty? That isn't like you. Did you do something wrong?"

"No, sir, I never," Shorty Joyner quickly said.

"This gentleman is a deputy United States marshal and he somehow got the idea that you are a witness in a shooting."

Shorty looked up at Longarm towering over him. He seemed mighty unhappy.

"You aren't in any trouble, Mr. Joyner," Longarm said. "I only wanted to ask about the night Ed Marsh was shot."

"That was more than a month ago. Why're you asking about it now?"

"It's a matter for the courts, y'see," Longarm told him. "I need to speak with all the witnesses."

Shorty seemed reluctant and still perhaps a little nervous. "Tell the marshal about it, Shorty," said Coburn. "You have nothing to hide, do you?"

"Not me, sir. Not exactly."

"Tell the marshal what you know then. Just tell him the truth."

"Yes, sir."

"That's all I want, Shorty. Just the truth," Longarm said.

"Okay, but I won't do you much good."

"The truth, whatever it is, is what will do me some good, Shorty."

"Yeah, well . . . I was there that night. That's true enough. It was my day off from work and I went in to shoot some billiards with a couple of the boys. I was at the billiards table scrunched down eyeballing the lay of things so's to line up my shot, and I heard this loud bang right behind me. It startled me so bad I dropped my cue stick and almost put a tear in the tabletop. They wouldn't of liked that. Anyhow, I turned around to see what was what and I seen Ed bent over, holding on to his belly with both hands. He had a gun out but he wasn't paying it no mind.

"There was a fat little fella about my height but real round, he was maybe ten feet away. He had a gun too.

"Then Ed, he gave out this long sigh . . . he was awful close to where I was standing so I could hear it plain . . . and he dropped down to his knees, still holding on to his gut. Next thing I knew he toppled over."

Shorty demonstrated with his hand how Marsh fell over onto his side. "Ed tried to say something, but there was blood running out of his mouth and he shit his pants and pretty soon his legs began shaking and the heels of his shoes pounding the floor and then he just . . . died.

"Someone in the crowd shouted murder. I looked around to see who did that. It was Charles Wynn. He shouted it again. Then I turned to see what the fat fella was doing but he was gone. I never seen him again. Never saw him before that night neither."

"The police report says that you saw the shooting, Shorty."

"Then Gary must've got me mixed up with somebody else 'cause I never saw either one of them shoot."

"Both of them fired?"

"No, there was only the one noise."

"But both men had guns in their hands," Longarm said.

"That's right."

"What happened to Marsh's pistol?" The official police report stated that Marsh was armed but that his revolver was secured in an underarm shoulder holster when the shooting was investigated.

"I'm not sure. I . . . I think maybe Charles picked it up and put it back in Ed's holster. Like to get it out of the way, you see. I remember for sure that Charles was the first one to go to Ed. It was Charles that rolled him over and felt for a pulse and like that. I guess . . . yes, I'm pretty sure Charles took the pistol out of Ed's hand and put it back out of the way."

"What kind of pistol was it, Shorty?"

"Oh, I wouldn't know about that. I don't know anything about guns. Never fired one, not my whole life long."

"Who is Charles Wynn, Shorty, and where can I find him?"

"Charles is a teller at the Manitou Bank and Trust. He's there every day. Never misses a day of work."

"Thank you, Shorty. You've been a big help." Longarm turned to go, then paused and turned back. "By the way, Shorty, did you write out the report about what you saw that evening? The police report, I mean?"

Shorty laughed. "Not me, Marshal. I can't read nor write, either one. Something about my eyes. I see the letters all mixed up somehow. I tried and tried but I just can't seem to learn how."

"All right. Thank you. Both of you."

Shorty Joyner and Phil Coburn went back to their own affairs. Longarm rattled down the stairs to the street and looked in both directions. He had another stop or two to make before he went to the bank to speak with Charles Wynn.

Chapter 34

"No, sirree, Marshal, not me. I didn't see nothing. I heard tell but I never seen anything."

"You were in the saloon that night, weren't you?"

"Oh, sure. I was there all right. I'm there most every night. But I was playing cards with my pals. I heard the shot and I seen Ed fall down, but I never seen whoever it was that shot him."

"What about Gary Cole? Was he there?"

"No. Gary was working that night. I think someone said it was Chief Anderson's night off or something like that. Gary, he came in later, after the shooting, and took over. Talked to everybody to get it straight in his mind what happened."

"Did he talk to you?"

"Yeah. He talked to me the next day."

"Did you write out a report for the police?"

"No, sir, I never done that."

"Did you sign the report Constable Cole wrote?"

"No, sir, I never done that either."

There was a witness report in Jim Anderson's files, ostensibly signed by this man. Longarm did not say anything about that.

"What about Charles Wynn?"

"He was there. Charles is there just about every night. For some reason he wasn't playing cards like he usually does." The man grinned. "That's a shame too. We all like to have Charles play at our table. He's a lousy poker player."

"Loses a lot, does he?"

"Yeah. Good thing he's a banker, else he likely couldn't afford to lose like he does."

Longarm grunted and spent a moment in deep thought. Finally he thanked the man, excused himself, and went back to the police headquarters and jail to go over those reports again and clarify a few things with John Handley.

"I saw the fat man shoot. I never saw who nor what he was shooting at until afterward. Wasn't no doubt that it was him did it, though, I can tell you that."

"And after the shooting. Did you see what the fat man did then, sir?"

"No. By then I heard Ed hit the floor. I turned and saw the crowd gathering around him. I never saw the fat man again after that moment."

"I wish I could be more help to you, Marshal, but I had my beak buried in a mug of beer at the time. I heard the shot. Turned around. Saw Ed drop. I never saw who fired the shot that killed him."

"It was some squatty little tub of lard that done it. Bald guy with a beard. I saw him shoot."

"Did you see Ed Marsh too?"

"Sure, but only after he was shot. I was looking toward the door, expecting a friend of mine who was late."

"And this fat man, he just walked in, saw Marsh . . .

172

or somebody . . . pulled his gun, and fired without provocation?"

"Without what, Marshal?"

"Without any reason to fire."

"Oh, I wouldn't know what reason he had. He walked in . . . I was watching the door, mind, so I saw him come in. He walked in, seemed like he was just coming in for a beer or something. Next thing you know he stopped and stiffened up. Scared, like. Then he came out with his gun slick as a duck on a June bug. I never saw anything so fast. Wouldn't have believed it was possible. And him such a lardass. You don't think of someone like that being fast with a gun, do you."

"No," Longarm agreed, "you don't. How did he look?"

"What do you mean, Marshal?"

"Did he look? You say he looked scared, but did he look angry too?"

The fellow thought about the question for a moment, then shook his head. "No, I wouldn't say he looked angry. Just scared. And startled."

"All right, thanks. You've been a big help."

"All I did, sir, was to tell you the truth about what I saw, and that was little enough."

"The truth is always a big help." Longarm smiled. "Sometimes pretty rare too."

The witness laughed. "Yeah, I know what you mean there."

Longarm started to leave, then paused. "One thing more. Did you write out a report about your experience that night?"

"No, sir. I talked with the constable but I didn't write anything down."

"Did he take notes or anything?"

"Not that I saw, but I wouldn't know if he wrote anything down later that night or anything."

"Did you sign anything?"

"No, sir."

Longarm nodded. "Thank you for your help, sir."

"Any time, Marshal. You know where to find me. I'm here every day, eight in the morning until six at night. I'm always glad to help out."

"I'm sorry, sir, the bank is about to close now. You will have to wait until morning. We will open at—"

"I'm not here t' do any banking."

The natty gent with a handsomely trimmed dark beard and an elk's-tooth dangler on a heavy gold watch chain seemed taken aback. He halted abruptly and peered at the revolver on Longarm's belt.

"I'm not here to rob the place either," Longarm assured him. He took out his wallet and displayed the badge there. "I need to see a gentleman named Charles Wynn."

"I am he. Is there some sort of trouble?"

"Oh, no. No trouble at all. I just need to talk with you. Clarify a few things in my mind."

"About what?"

"The murder of Ed Marsh. I understand you were there that night."

"That's right. But who are you? I know you are not a member of the town police force. I know all those gentlemen. So who are you and how is this any of your affair?"

"The deceased was an employee of the Post Office, Mr. Wynn, an agency of the United States government. Apart from having arrested the man who is accused of the crime, I need to make sure that shooting did not represent any sort o' threat to the Post Office or to the government."

"I see. Of course. Give me a moment to put the CLOSED sign in the window and lock the door. We can talk without interruption then."

174

"Good, thanks."

Wynn took the OPEN sign propped in the window and turned it around so that it read CLOSED from the outside; then he locked and bolted the heavy front doors. When he was done with that, he held up a finger and said, "Excuse me for one moment, please. I need to tell my employer."

"Sure." Longarm idled at the tall oak table where pens and inkwells had been placed along with a stack of deposit slips—but no withdrawal forms, Longarm noticed—for the convenience of the bank's customers. Wynn was gone only a few moments. Then he beckoned Longarm over to the side of the dark-paneled room where there were wooden armchairs along the wall.

The two sat side by side. Longarm crossed his legs and made himself comfortable. Wynn sat primly upright in his chair with his knees close together. "How may I help you, Marshal?"

"You can tell me about the events of that night, please."

"I have already gone over all this with Constable Cole. In fact, I wrote out a very complete accounting of everything I saw. That information was signed and given to the constable the next day."

"It's in the file. I've read it," Longarm allowed.

"Then you already know everything that I could possibly tell you."

"Would you mind going over it again, please."

"Not at all." Wynn proceeded to recite his report almost word for word, just as Longarm saw it in the police records. "I believe that is everything," he said when he was done.

An older gentleman with muttonchop whiskers came out from behind the teller windows and said, "Don't be too long here, Charles. We still have to complete the daily record before we close the vault."

"I won't be long, sir."

"See that you aren't." The old fellow withdrew without so much as acknowledging Longarm's existence. Let the snotty son of a bitch lose ten cents to a holdup and he would be singing a different song, Longarm thought. He wouldn't be so damned far above the likes of a lowly deputy marshal then.

"Can I get back to work now?"

"I only have a few more questions, Mr. Wynn."

"All right then."

"How much do you make?"

"Pardon me?"

"Your salary. How much are you paid as a teller in this bank?"

"Why do you need to know that?"

"Why would you want to hide it?"

"I don't want to hide it. It is just . . . a very personal and private matter, that is all."

"I can subpoena the bank's records if you prefer. You employer could be compelled to turn over all records for examination," Longarm said.

And technically he could do that. If there was good enough reason. And if he could find a judge who would go along with the request. Neither of those was a given, but both were certainly possible within the scope of the law.

"No, no, there is no, um, reason for that. I, uh, I earn, well, I make eight and a half dollars a week."

"That ain't much for a man with so much responsibility on his shoulders. A banker teller, why, you're a man of considerable stature in the community," Longarm said. "Seems a damn shame you get paid hardly more than a common cowhand."

Wynn snorted. "Tell my employer about it, would you."

"If I thought it would do any good, Mr. Wynn, I surely would."

The man seemed to relax a little. "Is there anything else?"

"No much. Now one thing I'm not clear on is about Ed Marsh's gun. He was wearing one, wasn't he?"

"Yes, he was, but he never took it out. That man just shot him down."

"For no reason?"

"If there was a reason, Marshal, I would have no way to know what it might have been."

"No, I suppose not. Was Marsh a friend of yours?"

"An acquaintance. As are most of the people in this community. The respectable people, that is. Nearly everyone does business here."

"Including the man who shot Marsh?"

"No. I never saw him before. Not that I recall."

"But you and Marsh were not particularly close?"

"No, not really."

"And he didn't take his pistol out?"

"No."

"What about you? D'you carry a pistol, Mr. Wynn?"

"Of course. I believe you will find that every banker does. Discreetly, of course."

"Of course. This bank here . . . d'you do much business with postal money orders?"

Wynn looked startled. "I . . . I . . ."

"You don't hafta answer that if you don't want to. Like I said, I can get the bank's records subpoenaed if it'd be more convenient for you."

"I . . . well . . . we do accept money orders. Of course we do."

"Do more business in them than most banks?" Longarm asked.

"I wouldn't know how much traffic other banks would have in them."

"But this bank does a good bit, does it?"

"I suppose you could say so. I would not know for sure."

Longarm stood. He smiled at the banker. But the smile did not reach as far as his eyes. "Thanks for your help, Mr. Wynn. I think I'll be seein' you again, sir. Real soon."

Charles Wynn was trembling. Sweat beaded his brow and a tic formed in his left eye.

"Somethin' wrong, Mr. Wynn?"

"No, I . . . no. Nothing is wrong."

Longarm turned to leave.

Before he reached the door to let himself out, he heard a high-pitched, keening squeal coming from Charles Wynn throat.

Longarm spun around and dropped into a crouch in time to see the banker clawing at his coat pocket, struggling to get a tiny, nickel-plated revolver out.

"Don't!" Longarm barked. "Leave it!"

His hand swept the big Colt .44-.40 out and brought it on line with Wynn's chest, but he needn't have made the effort.

Wynn tore his gun out—literally tore it, the pocket of his finely tailored suit ripping out in his urgency to draw the gun—and aimed it not at Longarm but back toward himself.

He shoved the muzzle of the pistol hard against the roof of his mouth and pulled the trigger.

"Oh, shit," Longarm muttered as a small pellet of lead smashed through bone and brain tissue, sending a fine red mist into the air above Wynn's head.

"Shit!" Longarm cursed again.

Chapter 35

"You're accusing me of murder, damn you?" The Manitou constable came halfway out of his chair, sudden rage turning his face beet red and making a most unpleasant contrast with his red hair.

"Set down, kid, an' keep your hand away from that hogleg or I'll take it away from you an' shove it up your ass," Longarm shot back at him.

"Sit down, Gary. Let's hear the man out," Chief Anderson cautioned his nephew-sort-of. "Are you sure about this?" Anderson asked of Longarm.

Longarm nodded. "An examination o' the bank records will bear it out with all the proof you're ever likely t' get, but I'm sure enough."

"But you are saying that I falsified my reports," Gary Cole protested. "That's a lie, you son of a bitch."

Longarm reached over and backhanded the constable across the mouth hard enough to knock his chair over and send Cole sprawling onto the floor.

"Touch that gun, sonny, an' I'll shoot your dick off. That's a promise."

"Be still, Gary. And if you have any small lick of sense left in that thick skull of yours," Anderson told him, "you won't call this man a son of a bitch again. That is fighting talk, and you are not man enough to back it up, sad to say."

Cole's glare was venomous, swiveling back and forth between Longarm and Jim Anderson. But he kept his hand well clear of his pistol. He climbed slowly back onto his feet and picked up the chair.

"What I was sayin', kid," Longarm went on, "is that you are lazy. You only had one good witness to that shooting, that was Charles Wynn, an' he was lyin' to you. Everyone else saw only a piece o' what happened. And none of them knew what brought it on."

"Why did Handley shoot Marsh then, Longarm?" Anderson asked.

"Pure self-defense," Longarm said. "Marsh intended t' murder Jack Handley cold and deliberate to keep him from sayin' anything to folks."

"About what?"

"That afternoon Handley was around the back o' the bank building looking in the trash for a rag to wipe the feet o' his paint horses. He was wanting to paint some hoof-black on them and didn't want t' ruin any of the piece o' cloth he had. He saw Marsh and Wynn there whispering to one another. Wynn had a bunch o' postal money orders in his hand. Handley didn't think anything of it. I only got it out of him by making me tell me every last detail of his stay here in Manitou, right down to where he took a crap.

"Him being there spooked Marsh an' Wynn only because they was up to something they oughtn't of done. Which was to steal from Wynn's bank an' split their loot."

"How could they steal from the bank?" Anderson asked. "I know good and well that Howard Teal balances his accounts each and every night. He insists that everything balance right to the penny."

180

"But it was Wynn that was doing the balancing, wasn't it?" Longarm said.

"I wouldn't know about that."

"I can almost guarantee it. Ask the banker and I'm betting you will find it so. Anyhow, Marsh would provide the money orders an' Wynn would cash them at the bank just like everything was on the up-and-up. Their problem was that the Post Office requires close audits of all postal accounts. They ain't a trusting bunch. The bank, on the other hand, took care o' their own books. So when Wynn was taking in the Post Office deposits, he wrote down more than was actually there.

"The Post Office books always balanced so they didn't see no reason to do anything, and the bank hadn't caught on to there being any shortage because they were dealing with numbers on paper instead o' actual cash an' money orders an' such, just relying on those deposit records that Wynn falsified."

Longarm shrugged. "That stupid son of a bitch Wynn panicked when I started talking about his bank taking in a lot o' money orders. When I said I could get the bank audited, that was too much for him. He knew he'd be caught. I guess he'd been worrying about prison, likely since before Jack Handley came along and queered their deal."

"But you accused me—"

"No, I never did, Cole. You didn't know nothing about it. You just are lazy an' no good but you ain't on the take. You had one witness . . . Wynn . . . an' he was part o' the problem. And you did falsify official records. Worse, you're no good at it. I caught onto that part easy enough."

Constable Cole stood and stormed out of the jail.

"That kid is a real piece o' shit," Longarm observed as he dipped two fingers into his vest in search of a match.

"He's my brother's stepson. What can I do?"

"I think what you'd best do now," Longarm said, "is open that cell an' let Jack Handley go. The only thing he's guilty of is defending hisself from two men that thought he could expose them for thieves."

"I am truly sorry, Longarm."

"Hell, Jim, you didn't do nothing wrong. Now let's you an' me go give Jack some good news about his future, eh?" Longarm nipped the twist off the tip of a cheroot and grinned.

He sobered again a moment later when he remembered Emily Balcomb. This trip had not been so complete a success after all, dammit.

Watch for

LONGARM AND THE DEADLY LOVER

the 334th novel in the exciting LONGARM
series from Jove

Coming in September!

GIANT-SIZED ADVENTURE FROM AVENGING ANGEL LONGARM.

LONGARM AND THE UNDERCOVER MOUNTIE
0-515-14017-1

THIS ALL-NEW, GIANT-SIZED ADVENTURE IN THE POPULAR ALL-ACTION SERIES PUTS THE "WILD" BACK IN THE WILD WEST.

U.S. MARSHAL CUSTIS LONG AND ROYAL CANADIAN MOUNTIE SEARGEANT FOSTER HAVE AN EVIL TOWN TO CLEAN UP—WHERE OUTLAWS INDULGE THEIR WICKED WAYS. BUT FIRST, THEY'LL HAVE TO STAY AHEAD OF THE MEANEST VIGILANTE COMMITTEE ANYBODY EVER RAN FROM.

AVAILABLE WHEREVER BOOKS ARE SOLD OR AT PENGUIN.COM

**Explore the exciting Old West with one
of the men who made it wild!**

Penguin Group (USA) Online

What will you be reading tomorrow?

Tom Clancy, Patricia Cornwell, W.E.B. Griffin,
Nora Roberts, William Gibson, Robin Cook,
Brian Jacques, Catherine Coulter, Stephen King,
Dean Koontz, Ken Follett, Clive Cussler,
Eric Jerome Dickey, John Sandford,
Terry McMillan, Sue Monk Kidd, Amy Tan,
John Berendt...

You'll find them all at
penguin.com

*Read excerpts and newsletters,
find tour schedules and reading group guides,
and enter contests.*

Subscribe to Penguin Group (USA) newsletters
and get an exclusive inside look
at exciting new titles and the authors you love
long before everyone else does.

PENGUIN GROUP (USA)
us.penguingroup.com